THE

BEST

FRIEND

An utterly addictive psychological suspense

SUSANNA BEARD

Joffe Books, London
www.joffebooks.com

First published in Great Britain in 2023

Cover art by Nick Castle

ISBN: 978-1-83526-016-6

For loyal friends, everywhere

PROLOGUE

Darkness fell quickly, the shadows around the garden concealing me from the house. Plenty of time to change my gardening hat to a baseball cap, my raincoat to a dark jacket. The finishing touch was a pair of leather gloves, and I was transformed into a proper cat burglar. I bundled the discarded clothes into the backpack and hid it beneath a bush.

Around six, as I expected, a figure emerged from the house. The side door opened. He paused for a moment to set the alarm — I heard a series of tones — and pulled the door closed behind him. He didn't bother with the second lock.

He was a big man, his stomach protruding over his trousers. I could tell by his walk he was unfit — he shambled rather than walked. A bright security light came on as he went down the drive and I could see he was dressed in a bomber jacket and ill-fitting trousers. His bald pate shone pink in the bright light, emphasising the ring of white hair around his head.

I would have to get rid of that light later.

I waited a few minutes to be sure he wasn't coming back, then I crept from my hiding-place, my trainers silent on the grass. I walked round the house, checking for security cameras. There were four. With my stick, I angled three out of four away from the house. The fourth, set high up on the top floor, I would have to avoid as far as I could. The security light was more of a problem — I had to disable it, but I couldn't reach. At the bottom of the garden, I found a shed, unlocked. I was looking for a wheelbarrow or a large pot I could upend to stand on, but straight away I spotted a small set of steps — exactly what I needed. That was careless. Nobody in their right mind would leave a stepladder in an unlocked shed. He'd become lazy. I suppose he thought nobody knew about the money.

Within minutes I'd stepped up to the light and smashed it with my stick. When he came back, he'd assume the bulb had blown or the light was malfunctioning. The likelihood of him investigating in the darkness after a few drinks was nil. I did the same with another security light on the back of the house, put the steps away exactly as I found them and returned to my den in the bushes, where I settled down to wait.

The time passed slowly, but it gave me a chance to consider all the angles. I was in no danger of falling asleep, given what I was about to do. My heartbeat was already so loud I was scared it would be heard by a passing pedestrian. I had a couple of hours to calm myself before he returned. But I stayed alert, ready for the moment. It came soon enough.

At the click of the opening gate, I got into a crouch and peered through the foliage. A dark figure tottered down the drive. Excellent. I needed him to be drunk, careless and a long way from alert. He fumbled with his key and went inside, the light from the hallway silhouetting him. A series of electronic beeps told me the alarm was disabled. That was the first hurdle crossed.

I crept to the back of the house where first one light, then the next, shone out from inside, illuminating the terrace. I'd checked out the sitting room in my first recce, and I was pretty sure that was where he'd settle down for the rest of the evening, hopefully with a strong drink to hand.

He didn't bother to close the curtains. Another small stroke of luck. I flattened myself against the wall and took a quick look inside the room. Sure enough, the TV was on, and I could see the green of a football pitch dotted with players. The sound of the crowd reached me through the windows. He was sprawled on a large sofa, his right leg stretched out on the cushions. One arm lay along the back of the sofa, and in his left hand was a large tumbler.

It was time for me to make a move.

CHAPTER 1

Alice

"Hello, Alice."

The person on the doorstep looks familiar, but for a moment I'm confused. I blink at the hooded figure standing hunched against the drizzle.

"Forgotten me already?"

I stare. Blue-grey eyes gaze back at me, dark shadows beneath. A layer of stubble on pale cheeks. Long nose, thin lips, a crooked smile. I can't see any hair under the hood of the rain-drenched coat.

"Carl?"

The figure laughs, a wide smile transforming the face. "Yes, it's me! Caught you for a moment, there, didn't I?"

"You did. You're the last person I was expecting to see." I'm transfixed by the sight of him.

"Aren't you going to let me in? It's chucking it down out here."

"I — — of course, sorry. Come in, Jason's in the living room." I stand back as he steps onto the doormat, stamping his feet. Water streams onto the floor.

"Here, let me take your coat. You're drenched."

I'm not impressed. It's ten o'clock and normally we'd turn in soon. Chances are, he's looking for a bed for the night. But I can't turn him away, not in weather like this.

I hook his coat behind the door where it drips onto the tiles. "Come through."

Jason's watching TV. I put my head round the door. "You have a visitor. It's Carl." I try to keep my voice steady.

"Carl?" His eyebrows raise. "*The* Carl?"

I nod, grimacing.

Jason jumps up, giving my hand a quick squeeze as Carl comes into the room. I turn off the TV, unspoken questions gathering in my head. *What does he want at this time of night? Is he going to stay? Why now?* There will be a reason, that's for sure, for him turning up after all this time.

"What can I get you, Carl?" I say. It's an effort not to grit my teeth. "Tea, coffee?"

Carl glances at Jason. "Maybe a beer?"

"Some at the back of the fridge," Jason says. "I'll have one too. Thanks, Alice." He gives me a grateful look. He knows how I feel about Carl.

As I prepare the drinks in the kitchen, the strains of South American salsa music reach me from the living room. There's always music in our house, courtesy of the best sound system we could afford when we got here.

I close the door for a moment, not because of the music but because I want to shut Carl out.

CHAPTER 2

Alice

When I return with the tray, they're sitting on opposite sides of the room. A look of surprise flits across Jason's face when I sit beside him. He knows I'd rather not spend time with Carl.

I watch Carl's face as his eyes flicker around the room. He nods approvingly at the bookshelves, the pictures on the walls.

"Great set up you've got here. Kids?"

"Not yet," Jason says, smiling at me. "We moved in together about four years ago."

"Nice."

Carl runs his fingers through his damp hair. "I needed to get out of that rain." He jumps up, stepping over to the window, where the curtains are half-shut. He peers into the darkness for a moment. "Yes, still pouring out there." But I get the impression it's not just the weather he's checking.

"So, Carl." Jason flips the top off his beer and pours it into a glass. "What brings you here after all this time?"

"Can't I visit an old friend — sorry, old friends—" he flashes a smile at me. I don't return it — "without a reason?" He takes a long draught of beer.

"Of course. It's good to see you." Jason hesitates. "But I am surprised. How long has it been? Nine, ten years?"

Carl shrugs. He taps his fingers against his beer bottle in time to the music. "Yeah, at least that long. But it's a spur-of-the-moment thing. Had a bit of time on my hands, so I thought I'd visit the old stamping ground, call in on some mates, spend a few days at my mum's."

"You've lost weight," Jason says.

It occurs to me that he's not looking well. I wonder what he's been doing, to look so run-down. Carl and Jason grew up together and of the two, Carl was always the robust one, his tall figure oozing confidence and health. Beside him, Jason looked like his little brother — smaller than him, always in his shadow. To be fair, he was younger by a couple of years.

But now Carl looks older than his age, thin, a little hunched, his trousers hanging off him. The skin on his face is grey, his once-lush hair dull and greasy.

"A bit. Too much burning the candle at both ends." Carl grins. He was always a late bird, always the one who found the next place to go to, the next party, the secret gathering where drink and drugs flowed.

"Same old Carl, then," Jason says. "What are you up to? Married, partner, kids? Job?"

"Nope, none of that. Still waiting for The One."

Jason snorts. "Don't give me that — you're too happy being single."

"You could say that. As for work, well . . ." Carl stretches, thin wrists appearing from the fraying cuffs of his jumper. "Bit of this, bit of that. Done some building work, labouring, you know. Worked in a casino for a while, that was a laugh. But it's better down here, in the big smoke. More lively, you know? Working for a tree surgeon. Not full time, but it's something."

"Sounds great. Better than being indoors all day, anyway. Can't quite imagine you in an office."

"Any more beer where that one came from?" Carl tips the bottle, his Adam's apple popping.

It's Jason's turn to go for the drinks, leaving me with Carl. There's a brief, awkward silence. I watch as he stands again and checks the street outside. "Something going on outside, Carl?" I say. It's as if he's expecting someone else to arrive.

"Just checking on the weather," he says, returning to his seat. But somehow, I don't believe him. It's my turn to go to the window. There's no movement outside. The street shines with wetness, the orange light of the street lamps reflecting off puddles on the pavement. A row of parked cars glistens through the rain. Pointedly, I close the curtains.

Jason returns with the beers, handing one to Carl. "You'd better stay over — you can't go back out in that."

"Brilliant — thanks, Jason. If it's not too much trouble." Carl glances over at me, but I don't meet his eyes. This is Carl all over. He knew we'd have to offer him a bed for the night.

Jason turns to me. "Alice, did you want another tea?"

"No thanks. I'm shattered — I'm going to turn in." Carl is clearly holding back — no doubt because of me. I'll get the real news from Jason later.

"You don't look tired at all," Carl says. "You look pretty good to me."

"Thanks." I don't meet his eyes. He won't get round me the way he does with other people. "I'll say goodnight — leave you two to catch up."

"Okay, love, see you up there." Jason touches my hand as I leave the room.

"Yes. Night, Carl."

"Night, Alice."

The rain drums on the roof, droplets running down the skylight above the stairs. It lets the light in during the day and frames the stars on a clear night. But not tonight.

CHAPTER 3

Alice

As I pad around the bedroom, preparing for bed, my mood worsens. Carl turning up unannounced late at night can only mean bad things. I peer out of the window again, wondering what that was all about, but there's no movement. No cars feeling their way down the street, no dark figures lingering across the road.

But there's no doubt Carl was jumpy. I wonder if he thinks he's being followed — in which case he's in trouble again. Some things never change.

I wonder — not for the first time — how two characters so different in nature could become close friends. It always seemed to me an unlikely fit. Perhaps it was simply habit, or history. Carl and Jason were close as children, almost like brothers. They lived nearby, shared a seat on the school bus, were in and out of each other's houses as they grew up. I was at the same school, though not in the same class as either of them. When I started going out with Jason at seventeen, Carl was part of the package.

I didn't mind, at first. Carl was a bit of a clown, endearing and funny — he was good company. In some ways he was charming, and I liked him. But there was another side to him, one that slowly revealed itself as I got to know him better. I began to wonder why Jason was so loyal to a friend who let him down so often, so badly. He never complained about him. There seemed to be something binding Jason to Carl that I didn't know or understand.

Once I asked why he put up with him. His jaw tightened, but he answered simply: "He's my friend, and I owe him." He didn't say why, and his face closed.

I never asked again.

With a sigh, I climb into bed and make an effort to read my book. But my mind returns to Carl, and what has brought him here so unexpectedly, so late in the evening and after all this time. I hope Jason gets to the bottom of it and tells me all when he eventually comes to bed. But I'm tired, and the muffled voices downstairs drone on. It will have to wait until morning, whatever it is.

I'm not looking forward to seeing Carl tomorrow. He'll hang around while we get ready for work, and I wouldn't be surprised if he angles to stay for longer. I'm really not keen on having him stay at all — not even for a few days. He has a way of getting people to cater for him, and I'm not doing that. Luckily Jason knows how I feel. He'll know I don't want Carl here a minute longer than necessary.

Tomorrow I'll make sure he leaves when we do. Who knows what he might get up to, left to his own devices in our house.

* * *

In the morning, I ask Jason what's going on with Carl.

"Nothing," he says.

I give him a sideways glance.

"Nothing he revealed last night, anyway. Though I got the impression he was holding back. I could have pushed him, but I wanted to get to bed. I didn't want to get into some big story about his life at that time of night."

"Hm. There'll be something that's brought him here, I'm sure of it. Probably wants money."

"We haven't got any, so that's easy to deal with."

I smile. "Right. But, Jason, please don't let him stay any longer. One night is fine, but no more."

He gives me a hug. "Don't worry, I don't want him here any more than you do. He'll be off to his mum's today. Now, I need a shower."

When I get downstairs, Carl's already there in the kitchen, greeting me with a cheery "Morning!"

I manage a weak smile. "Morning, Carl. Sleep well?"

"I did indeed, thank you — very comfortable bed in your spare room, I must say. Out like a light, I was." Carl leans on the worktop, letting me step around him as I reach for mugs, cutlery and dishes for breakfast. I hope Jason will be quick in the shower. I like to be quiet and relaxed in the mornings, waking up slowly. But today I can feel the tension in my shoulders, in my lower back. Carl has a way of doing this to me.

"Tea or coffee?" I say. "We normally grab some toast and get going. Can I put some on for you?"

"Coffee please. Yeah, great, toast is perfect. Can I do anything?" He's still lounging against the cupboard.

"Sit down, I've got this."

Carl sits, yawns and stretches. "What are you up to these days, then, Alice?"

"I'm in marketing. I work in Chiswick." I place a steaming cup of coffee and some milk in front of Carl.

"Nice. Enjoy it?" He looks about as interested in my work as I am in chicken farming.

At that moment, Jason walks into the kitchen, bringing with him the aroma of coconut shampoo, his fair hair slicked back. It's thick and getting long, curling at the neck now, with a lock that falls across his face on one side. Slim and neat in a blue jumper, jeans and sneakers, he looks about eighteen years old.

"Morning, mate," he says, clapping Carl on the shoulder as he passes. He comes to my side, kissing the top of my head. "Hi, you, all okay?"

I smile and nod, turning to put a plate of toast on the table. "Help yourself, Carl, there's butter and marmalade, honey and Marmite. Take your pick."

"Lovely."

"Listen, I'm going in ten minutes. Do you want a lift anywhere, Carl?" I catch Jason's eye. He gives me a small nod of acknowledgement — he knows I don't want to leave Carl in the house. I'm thankful that he understands me, even if he does have a friend who's the opposite of sensitive.

"No, I'm fine thanks. I'll wander over to Mum's a bit later."

"It's pouring with rain out there. I'm taking the car to the tube station today — I'll drop you off." Jason makes it sound like a decision. "You don't want to get soaked all over again, your coat's only just dried off."

Carl shrugs. "If you insist, then."

I breathe a silent sigh of relief.

CHAPTER 4

Jason

"Drink after work at the Old Fox, then?"

"You haven't changed," Jason says.

"It'll be great to visit the old watering hole. I bet it's a bit different now."

"It's okay — the food's not bad. It's busy, especially at weekends."

Carl grimaces. "I hope it hasn't become one of those trendy places. I kind of liked it grubby and old-fashioned."

"It needed an update. It's better now."

"So, you're up for it later then?"

"Yeah, okay, a quick one. But I don't finish until at least seven."

"Seven? That's a long day. But you always were a grafter. Okay, I'll be there — I'll grab a drink if you're late."

Jason double-parks the car. Carl reaches for the door, then hesitates. "See you later then. There's something I want to talk to you about, so let's make it just the two of us, eh?"

"Sure."

With a wave, Carl's gone, leaving Jason wondering what's going on. It sounds ominous — he clearly doesn't want Alice there. Probably one of Carl's mad schemes, and he'll want Jason involved.

* * *

It's past seven thirty by the time he reaches the Old Fox. The place is quiet, only one or two people talking at the bar. Carl's hunched in a corner, studying his phone, a half-empty beer glass on the table. When he looks up, it's hard to miss the angry bruising around one eye, the cut high up on his cheek.

Jason removes his rain-spattered coat, pulls up a stool. "Sorry I'm late. What happened to you?"

Carl fingers the area around his eye. "It's nothing."

"Doesn't look like nothing."

"You should see the other guy." He grins, a cheerless curling of his lip. "Let me get you a drink."

"A half, thanks."

"What? Go on, make it a pint."

"No, really, I can't stop for too long."

"Alice got you under the thumb, eh?"

Jason suppresses a stab of annoyance. Alice isn't like that, and Carl knows it. But he's always had a knack of winding him up.

"So, what is it you wanted to talk about?" Jason says, as Carl returns with the drinks. Might as well get to the point.

Carl's expression is serious. "I'm in a bit of a corner, since you mention it," he says.

Jason feels the energy drain from his body.

"Go on then, tell me."

Carl takes a furtive look over his shoulder, though the tables around them are unoccupied. "I'm a bit short of money," he says, his fingers tracing shapes in the beer stains on the table. He seems unable to make eye contact.

"What, the job with the tree surgeon not working out?"

"There's not a lot of work at the moment for tree surgeons. It's the wrong time of year. There's a job probably every couple of weeks, but the money's not enough to live on. I'm on the benefit, too."

This sounds familiar. "Sorry to hear that. Have you looked for something better?"

Carl shakes his head. "I could get another job, keep myself going. But it wouldn't be much help. I've got to pay back a loan."

"A loan? What for?"

"It doesn't matter what it was for. But it's a lot, and I can't just go to the bank, there's no way they'd lend me anything, not right now. I don't have a proper salary, no assets — not even a proper fixed address." Carl glances up at Jason.

"What are you going to do, then?" Jason can guess what's coming next, but he wants Carl to say it.

"Listen, mate — can you help me out?" Jason begins to shake his head, but Carl goes on, the words rushing out now. "I don't mean you have to give me your savings — that's if you have any — but you have a proper job, a mortgage. You could get a loan, easy. I'll pay you back on a regular basis, I promise. Even if I have to get three jobs. I won't let you down."

Jason almost laughs. If there's one thing he knows about Carl, it's that he always lets you down. He shakes his head. "Carl. Mate. I don't have any money. Neither does Alice."

A look of disbelief passes over Carl's face. "But — you've got that nice house, you've both got steady jobs—"

"It's not like that, Carl."

Carl's voice drops now, and he leans forward, a desperate look in his eyes. "Look, I don't like to ask, you know I wouldn't unless it was important — but I really need this. I need your help here."

Jason hesitates. What he wants to say is that it's out of the question, that Carl's the last person he or anyone in their right mind would ever lend money to. Alice would blow a gasket. But there's no point. Speaking the truth would only lead to bad feeling.

"I know you're serious, and I'd like to help, I really would. But what I mean is, we don't have any money. We saved for ages to get the deposit for the house. We both have a salary, yes, but the mortgage takes up all the extra. We're barely keeping our heads above water. There's no way the bank would lend us any more. It's hard enough as it is."

Carl snorts, shaking his head. "Jason, please — I'm not just serious, I'm desperate. And there's no one else. You're the only person I know who could help. We go back a long way, we're mates. Please, I'm begging you."

Jason feels a flush crawl up his neck. He's never dealt well with confrontation. This is too much. Carl is pushing too hard. "No," he says. "I mean it. I can't get you any money, or lend you any money. If there's anything else I can do—"

Carl stares at Jason for a moment, then looks away.

"Does this have anything to do with—" Jason nods towards the injured eye. The purple swelling seems to be getting worse.

Carl avoids his gaze. "Maybe."

"Are you being threatened? Because if you are, you should tell the police. That's what they're for. And listen, Carl, there are ways of dealing with debt. I don't know how much you owe, or who you owe it to, but Citizen's Advice—"

Carl snorts. "Citizen's Advice? Police? Forget it, mate, we're not talking about Toy Town here. This is serious, and it's not going to go away. I've got to go." He downs the last of his drink and stands.

Jason watches as he walks away, his shoulders hunched. At the door, he pauses and turns, a strange expression on his face. "Think about it, Jason. You owe me."

The door swishes closed behind him.

CHAPTER 5

Jason

Though he knew it was coming, it's still a jolt in the gut. It's what kept him loyal to Carl for all those years. *You owe me.* But they're adults now, both of them. Years have passed without it coming back to visit him, but still it triggers those feelings of helplessness and inevitability that dogged him throughout his teenage years.

All the old feelings come rushing back. There were always elements of danger about Carl. Jason knew it then and he knows it now, so why does he feel so let down? Perhaps, without knowing it, he was hoping Carl might be different now. Stupid of him — of course he hasn't changed.

But what's this feeling of guilt? There's no reason at all for Jason to feel guilty. Carl waltzes into his life again after all these years, and almost the first thing he does is ask for money. Why should Jason have expected anything else? He learned his lesson early on. Lending money to friends is not a good idea — especially if they're Carl. You'll never see the money again.

But from the look in Carl's eyes, he's in deep trouble this time. There's no point wondering what he's done — it

16

will only confirm Carl's recklessness, his eternal, misplaced optimism.

Jason knows he hasn't heard the end of it yet. That comment when Carl left the pub: *Think about it* — that's a bad sign. Let alone *You owe me*. Carl can be relentless when he wants something; he can be hard to refuse. It's a good thing that Jason genuinely has no money to spare. If not, there's a danger he might give in, despite everything.

No lights greet him as he opens the door. He dislikes coming home to an empty house, but he's not surprised that Alice is late. She's probably met a friend for a drink on the way home, knowing he wouldn't be back on time. It's probably just as well. Alice will be furious if Jason tells her what Carl wants — even though he's said no.

Perhaps it's best not to tell her at all.

CHAPTER 6

Alice

Annoyance stabs at me when I see Jason's text. He doesn't go out a lot — he's a home-loving type, not one to spend hours in the pub with his friends, or to leave me wondering what he's doing. It's one of the reasons I love him. He's reliable, honest and kind — and he's my best friend. I trust him implicitly.

But if anyone can lead Jason astray, it's Carl — there's plenty of evidence for that.

It's already five o'clock. I gaze at the text for a moment. Outside, driving rain spatters the window. The tree across the street bends its long fingers to one side, as if reaching out for someone. The only place I want to be this evening is home in front of the fire and the television. With Jason by my side.

I sigh and type: *OK. Will try not to eat all the supper. See you later x*

A dull ache forms in the pit of my stomach, like a premonition. Though I attempt to get back to my work, it's hard to focus. I find myself reading the same page over and over without taking anything in. Perhaps I should call it a day, go home now. But despite the pull of a warm sofa, I'm restless. If Jason's going to be late, perhaps I should find a friend too.

An idea strikes me. I text: *Hi Dawn, are you up for a visit in about half an hour? Just me! X*

The answer comes straight back. *Of course! Will put the kettle on x*

Dawn and I have always been close. Though she's effectively my mother-in-law, it doesn't feel like that kind of relationship. As a teenager, I was always in and out of her home, often stopping for a chat, and the habit stuck when Jason and I bought our house around the corner. My parents moved to Devon when my sister and I left home a few years ago, and the journey there means I see Dawn more than I see them.

A side path, dotted with puddles, leads to the back door. I shake my umbrella outside, the droplets spattering my coat. Dawn always leaves the door on the latch when she's home. This part of London is relatively safe, with its interlocking streets of seventies houses, leafy parks and suburban lines of unprepossessing shops — a mini-supermarket, a hairdressers, a chemist, sometimes a small cafe. Time seems to have stopped here, the developers yet to notice its charms: proximity to the city centre, the quiet location. The locals like it this way, blocking all attempts to update the area.

Dawn works part-time at the local library, my favourite place to sit and read as a child. It's not changed much either, except for the addition of screens and more modern toys in the children's area. I still go there sometimes when I need a quiet moment.

"Dawn, I'm here!" I lean my umbrella in the corner by the back door, slipping off my damp coat. "Where are you?"

She appears at the kitchen door, her feet silent in rubber-soled pumps. She's a small woman in her fifties with shoulder-length blonde hair, often clipped back into a messy bun. "Hi, Alice — you surprised me. I didn't hear anything. Must be the wind."

"It's hideous out there." I remove shoes dark with moisture. My feet feel damp, my socks sticking to my toes.

"Come into the sitting room, it's warmer in there. I've got the fire on. Tea's already on the table."

"Fabulous — you're a star."

"Jason still at work, is he?" Dawn pours from a teapot into generous mugs.

"Right now, yes, I imagine. He's going for a drink later."

"With his workmates?" Dawn settles back into an armchair with a mug of tea.

I hesitate for a moment. "Actually, he's meeting Carl."

I watch the expression on Dawn's face as she places her mug carefully on a side table beside her. Though she's hard to read, the action takes a little too long.

"Carl? I haven't heard about him in a long time. Where's he been these last years?"

I shrug. "He hasn't changed. Never complain, never explain. Well, never explain, anyway. I have no clue where he's been. I'm not interested, either."

"Still not a fan, then?"

"No, I'm not. He turns up at bedtime last night, the same old Carl — and guess what? — stays the night. Jason couldn't exactly turn him out into the storm, could he? So, Jason's late to bed, tired this morning, and Carl's as bright as a button, angling for a lie-in at our house."

"I see."

"I know I'm not very generous when it comes to Carl, but I can't help it. The same old super-friendly, utterly unreliable old Carl. I don't get why anyone's taken in by him. He's never done anything for Jason — except get him into trouble."

"I know what you mean," Dawn says. "But they were good for each other when they were small."

"They were both an only child, weren't they? That must have brought them together."

"Indeed. It was nice for Jason to have another kid to play with when he was little. But things changed a bit when they were teenagers. At that age, you have to let them find their feet, you can't restrict them too much. They got closer, and Jason looked up to Carl. I suppose he was older, more confident . . ."

"Carl's never had a confidence problem in his life, I'll bet," I say.

"He was certainly a streetwise kid. Jason found him exciting." Dawn pauses. "I wasn't against Carl, though — in fact, I liked him. He was always friendly and polite, asking how I was, offering to help when he came to tea. But I worried about his influence on Jason."

"I'm not surprised — I would have done too."

"He was a boy of two sides, that's for sure. On the one side, charming, on the other, he had this wild, adventurous streak."

"I remember it well. Some of the things he got up to! Jason got roped in so often, and always regretted it."

Dawn sighs. "Indeed. And eventually, the adventurous streak went too far."

"It seems to me Carl was always going too far." But I'm intrigued. Maybe something happened that would explain the tie between the two men. "Was there a particular incident?"

She hesitates. "There was this one time when one of Carl's stupid pranks went wrong — badly wrong — and Jason got the worst of it. But he would never hear a word against Carl. They carried on being good friends as if nothing had happened."

I nod. But I get the distinct impression there was more to the incident than she's telling me.

CHAPTER 7

Alice

We hear nothing from Carl for a few days, and I secretly hope he's gone away again. But tonight, as we sit together in the living room, music playing in the background, Jason is unusually quiet, falling into long periods of thought. I can't help suspecting that Carl has something to do with it. After the third or fourth time that Jason seems not to hear me, I decide to find out.

"You seem distracted. Anything bothering you?"

"What? Oh. No, nothing. Just a bit . . . tired, I suppose." I can tell he's not concentrating. He's been fidgeting for the last half hour. He picks up his mobile, stares at it for a moment, then drops it on the sofa beside him.

"Heard from Carl again?" I try to make the question sound innocent and fail. My voice, even to me, sounds false.

He puts the iPad down, a shadow falling across his face. I can't read him and that worries me.

"One or two texts," he says. "He keeps asking me to go for a drink, but, you know, it's not my thing. The pub, every night — I've grown out of that."

"So, he's still around then?" I know I'm pushing him, but I need to know. "Staying at his mum's?"

"Yeah, I think so."

"You think so, or you know?" My heart gives a warning beat.

This is what Carl does. He gets in the way, confuses people. One minute he's the best friend, generous and amusing, the next, it's all gone wrong. Things are never . . . *normal* . . . when he's around.

I'm surprised when Jason stands up and strides towards the door.

"Look, he is still around, otherwise he wouldn't be asking me for a drink, would he?"

"But—"

"But nothing. I'm going for a run."

My shoulders sag, but I hold back.

A few moments later, I hear his feet on the stairs.

"See you in a bit," he calls. The front door opens and closes.

I sit for a moment or two, unhappy that we've left it like that. This doesn't feel right. There's something I don't know about what's going on between Jason and Carl. It's bothering Jason and I need to know about it.

My gaze lands on his mobile. It's against my principles but anxiety makes me pick it up, punch in the code and take a look. I remind myself that I'd be angry if Jason checked my messages — but I only hesitate a moment.

Come on, Jason, you have to help me. C

Jason replies: *I told you, I can't. There is no money.*

I feel the blood drain from my face. So, he's trying to get money from Jason, and this is what's bothering him. Somehow, the fact that Jason's refusing doesn't comfort me.

We need to meet. You owe me. This text arrived just before Jason left for his run. There's no reply. What does Jason owe him? That's a threat in my book, and I have a horrible feeling about it.

When Jason returns after almost an hour, the sweat dripping down his face, he puts his head around the door. I'm sitting in my usual armchair with a book. His mobile is on the sofa where he left it.

"I'm sorry, Alice."

"What for?"

"Carl. You're right, he's still around, and he's taking up far too much of my energy. As always."

I swallow. "What does he want from you, Jason? I know there's something."

He sighs, wiping the sweat away with a towel. "You won't be surprised. He's after money."

"Please don't give him anything."

"Don't worry — I've told him we've got no money, and I have no intention of borrowing it for him, believe me. But he insists I'm the only person who can help."

I suppress a snort of derision. "Of course he does! I bet he says that to everyone he knows when he wants something. He's manipulating you, taking advantage of your better nature. You're a decent bloke with a big heart, and you want to help him. You need to give yourself a break, or he'll never let you go."

"I've already told him I can't help him — in no uncertain terms."

"Let's hope he believes you, though I wouldn't bet on it. What does he want the money for?"

"He says he needs to pay back a loan, but I don't know who to. Or what it was for. I don't even know how much he needs."

Jason runs his hands through his sweat-soaked hair. I can tell from the look in his eyes there's a struggle going on in his head. "But?"

"He seems desperate, Alice. He's still a mate, and I'd like to help him."

Relief turns back into concern. "But how can you do that?"

Jason shrugs. "I can listen, give him my advice, be there for him. It's not much, but it's something."

24

"You're a good man, Jason."

What I want to say is *No, Jason! He's bad news. Keep away from him or there'll be trouble!*

I've already had too much trouble in my life, and I never want to go there again.

CHAPTER 8

Jason

"Look, I'm here, but it doesn't mean I can get you any money. And I don't have much time, sorry. One drink, and then I need to go."

Carl grins. The swelling around his eye has subsided, leaving only a dark smudge, its edges turning into a yellow stain on the pale skin of his cheek. "Thanks for coming."

"I mean it, Carl. I'll help you if I can, but not with money."

Carl taps a rhythm on the table with his fingers. They're back in the Old Fox. It's a Thursday night, one of the more popular nights of the week, and people are already gathering after work.

"You see, the thing is, Jason, I'm scared. I've really done it this time."

Startled, Jason watches his face. Carl is never scared — or at least, he's never admitted it.

"You're scared — of what?"

"Not what — it's who. This loan—"

"Ah, the loan. You haven't told me what it was for."

Carl shifts in his seat, glances over his shoulder. Nobody else is taking any notice of the two men sitting in the corner. "I got involved in this property deal in the Caribbean—"

Jason flinches. "What? Did you say 'in the Caribbean'?"

"I know it sounds too good to be true. But it looked brilliant, you know, beautiful place, practically on the beach, bona fide developer building luxury villas. Swanky brochures, professional website, lots of experience with other developments. Great return on investment — they said I'd get my money back, and more, in the first couple of years . . ."

It's not hard to guess what's coming. "So, it didn't work out." He keeps his voice flat.

"A few months in, the developer went bust, disappeared with the money. All of it, gone. No website, the phone's dead, emails bounced. Don't say anything, please. I know it was stupid. I wanted to get away, change my life, live in the sun for a while . . ."

"Oh, Carl." There's really nothing else to say.

"Yeah, well. But the thing is — the person who lent me the money, he's kind of a mate — or he was. He's cash-rich, always throwing money around."

"So, you thought you'd have a bit of it? And now he wants his money back? Of course he does." Jason can just imagine what Carl's "kind of a mate" is like.

Carl nods. "He's hard core — drugs and that. I didn't know, I thought he'd done well for himself, inherited money or something."

Jason wants to shake Carl for being such an idiot, tell him how obvious it is, how did he not see it coming, how did he get himself into such a mess? But he doesn't say any of it. There's no point.

"What precisely do you mean: 'hard core'?"

Carl shakes his head. "Christ, I'm such an idiot, Jason. I don't know why I did it. This bloke — let's call him Nick — he's got minders. Minders, I tell you!"

"Was the black eye down to him?"

Carl nods. "One of his guys caught up with me. He would have done a lot worse, but he grabbed me by the jacket. I was lucky — it came off and I ran. Had to abandon the jacket — it was a good one, too."

"This sounds bad, Carl. Can't you talk to him, persuade him to give you more time?"

Carl scoffs. "He's not that kind of guy — talking's not his way."

"So, tell me about him."

"It's not just him. There's a whole family of them in West London. They're into all kinds of shit — protection, trafficking, drugs, casinos — you name it. All round the world — it's huge. How did I not see it? Now he's got me over a barrel, and he's as hard as nails, won't listen to any excuses." Carl's eyes flicker. He swallows, a strangled groan escaping from his thin lips.

This is ten times worse than Jason could have imagined. Carl might be flaky but he's no hard criminal. He pushes the boundaries — always — but never quite flips over into crime.

"How much, Carl?"

Carl's foot taps, his eyes flitting as he checks the room out. More people have drifted in. A large group at the bar are laughing and talking. A couple sit at the window table, deep in conversation, but there's nobody close enough to hear.

"Nick. He's called Nick — he's loaded. It's a drop in the ocean to him," Carl says. "But he's like a dog with a bone in business. Never lets anyone get one over on him."

"Come on, Carl, how much?"

Carl's voice drops to a hoarse whisper. "A hundred grand. And if you say anything about how *stupid* I am . . ."

For a moment, Jason's stunned into silence. *What?? A hundred thousand pounds? What was he thinking?* But Carl's watching, a desperate look on his face.

"When? When are you supposed to pay it back?"

"Last month. They're after me, Jason, and if they catch me again, they'll fucking *kill* me."

CHAPTER 9

Jason

It's hard to imagine a worse scenario. An old friend, feckless but on the whole harmless, gets conned into investing in a "dream" property scheme on a Caribbean island. He borrows the money — a huge amount, for almost anyone — on the promise that his investment will be returned in record time. Almost certainly no legal papers, no formal agreement. The lender, a so-called "friend", turns out to be a ruthless criminal — quite possibly a gang leader — who rules by aggression and violence.

Carl watches Jason, waiting for his reaction. But Jason can't find the words. It's a huge amount of money — far more than he expected, and more than Carl can possibly hope to pay back, especially with his job history.

"Jason, you have to help me. I've got no hope of getting the money together. I don't have any savings — nothing. Mum's no use — I don't mean she's useless, but she has no money either. She has the house, and I know she'd offer to sell it, but I can't — I won't — ask her to do that. It's the only thing she has. I can't even tell her about this, it would kill her. I'm desperate, Jason — I don't know what to do."

"Shit, Carl!" He's still reeling.

"I know." Carl drops his chin to his chest.

Jason keeps his voice steady with some difficulty. "I don't know what to say, I really don't. Did I hear you right — a hundred thousand?"

"Keep your voice down." Carl takes a nervous look over his shoulder. But still nobody's close enough to hear.

Jason takes a deep breath. "Okay, let's think this through. Where are you living, officially?"

"I'm renting a room in Acton. It's cheap, nothing special. But they've tracked me down — I can't go back there. I've given notice. I've been couch-surfing and living rough for the last few weeks, trying to keep my head down. I daren't stay at Mum's for much longer. I can't put her in danger."

Jason can't help feeling angry with Carl for asking him to help. What does he think he can do? Jason's always been as straight as a die, except when Carl led him astray. But that was years ago, before he grew up. He likes his job; he's happy with his life with Alice. He doesn't need this kind of drama. The dark world of criminal gangs and violence is like a foreign land, something he's only seen on TV.

He shakes his head. "I want to help you, Carl, believe me. I know you saved me once, but—"

"Yes, I did, Jason. And now you need to save me."

CHAPTER 10

Alice

Jason's meeting Carl again, and I'm trying not to care. It's not that I don't trust Jason, it's that Carl is the most manipulative person I've ever met.

I throw on my joggers, put some music on and try to get Carl out of my mind. Supper's just about ready when I hear Jason's key in the lock. "In here!" I call.

"Smells good," he says, putting his head around the kitchen door.

"Almost done." I lift my chin for a kiss. Then I notice the look on his face. "Are you okay? You look kind of — shell-shocked." The skin on his face is grey; the lines on his forehead seem to have deepened. What's Carl been up to this time? I want to say it out loud, but Jason knows I'm suspicious. I don't want to come across like the jealous woman.

Jason's eyes skitter away from mine. "It's been a long day."

"And Carl? Did you see him?"

"I did." He sits at the table, runs his hands through his hair. It looks like a hopeless gesture, as if he doesn't know what to do.

"And?"

"It's bad. I'm not sure I should tell you, it's so bad."

I knew it. "Tell me."

"This loan he mentioned. He borrowed a lot of money from a very bad guy. Some kind of criminal gang leader, who's threatening him. He's really scared this time, Alice . . . I've never seen him like this before."

"Wow. Carl, scared — must be bad." I try to make light of it, but Jason's face is serious.

"I think it is. I don't know how to help him."

"Are they violent?"

"Just a bit. He thinks he's going to end up in the river with his throat slit."

CHAPTER 11

Alice

Jason picks up his phone and stares. He makes a strangled noise and holds it up for me to see.

Eight messages from Carl. I can almost feel Jason's stress levels rocket. Something bad must have happened — nobody sends eight messages in quick succession unless it's urgent.

The first message says simply: *This is bad. Call me.* The next: *Call me, ASAP!!* The messages get increasingly panicky, until the last one. *Ditching this phone. I'll call you.* There are six missed calls — all from Carl.

Once again, the colour drains from Jason's face.

"Try him," I say. There's no point telling Jason to ignore the messages. He taps the screen and waits, his eyes wandering around the room. "No answer. I reckon he's ditched it."

"Doesn't sound good, does it?" Jason paces the room. "I don't know what to do, Alice. What if he's in real danger? I've got to help him."

"Where's he likely to go?"

"He'll have left his mum's — he won't want to put her in danger. He could be sleeping rough."

"But where?" There are so many places in London he could be. Searching for him could be never-ending.

"I don't know. The railway line, maybe — we used to hang out there. Or the subway. Alice, I've got to go and look." When he looks at me, his eyes are anxious, appealing.

"I know. Be careful, though, won't you? And keep in touch."

He grabs his phone and his keys. "I will."

"Want me to call anyone? What about his mum?"

"Don't worry — I'll start there." Carl's mum, Julie, lives just around the corner. "I won't scare her, I'll find some excuse for needing to see him."

"If you find him, bring him here. But please—"

"Don't worry, I'll make it crystal clear. He can't stay for long."

I nod, blow him a kiss. A moment later, the front door slams.

I hate the idea of Jason out on his own, searching the streets of West London in the dark. But trying to stop him is useless. Jason is a rescuer, always has been, and now he's trying to rescue Carl. Though to be fair, it does sound as if Carl really is in need of rescuing this time.

I wonder what you do, ultimately, when you owe a lot of money and you have absolutely no chance of paying it back. Worse, if the people you owe it to are dangerous — and you can't go to the police.

I fear Carl might have to disappear for good.

CHAPTER 12

Jason

Jason climbs into the car, shivering in the damp air. This was not what he had planned for the evening. But he must find Carl.

If he draws a blank with Julie, Carl's mum, he'll check out their teenage haunts: the old railway line, the playing fields, the skate park. Then the places where the homeless hang out. Not that he knows where to go, but he can take an educated guess. Perhaps there's a hostel of some kind. Or maybe Carl's holed up in a deserted building. A scene from a film flits through his mind. A man on the run . . . empty warehouses, derelict factories. Is it worth checking them too? If he can find any. He's never noticed such places in the local area, but in London they're not unusual.

What else can he do? If he goes to the police, he risks landing Carl in trouble.

Carl's mum opens the door as far as its chain will allow, peering through the gap with wary eyes. "Jason?"

"Hi, Julie. Yeah, it's me."

"Come in, quick, close the door." She looks out into the street, checking in both directions before turning back to him.

35

"Is everything okay?"

"Fine, fine. Come through."

She gives him a swift hug before leading him down the hallway. She seems smaller than when he last saw her, though her step is firm, her movements quick and efficient, her dark hair pulled back into a thick ponytail.

"I'd love to join you," he says, nodding at the steaming mug on the kitchen table. "But it's only a quick visit. I'm looking for Carl."

"Aren't they all?" she says, almost to herself. She points him to a chair and sits opposite. The kitchen is barely big enough for a table. It's exactly as it was fifteen years ago — the same cracked tiles on the floor, the same pine cupboards. Neat and clean, and like a picture from the past.

"What, has someone else been here?" He tries to keep the dismay from his face.

"Two blokes, one smart-ish, the other bald, in jeans. Heavy-looking fellow. Luckily, I saw them from my bed-room window. Right away, I was suspicious. I pretended to be out, didn't open the door. They nearly smashed it in, yelled to Carl through the letter-box. I was scared — I hid for a full half hour after they'd gone."

"What did they say?"

"Told Carl to watch out, they're coming for him, something like that."

"Did you see their faces?"

"Not clearly. I watched as they left — they got into a car parked down the road and drove off."

"When was this?"

"About six o'clock yesterday evening. I was lucky to spot them under the streetlights. I don't know what would have happened if I'd let them in."

He hesitates. "Julie — I don't want to scare you, but don't open the door to anyone unless you know who they are, okay? What are your neighbours like?"

"Good people — friends."

"Call them. Tell them what's happened, ask them to be vigilant, to note anything strange. If you're really worried, is there anywhere you can go?"

She gives him a look. "I'm not going to be chased out of my house, Jason, not easily, anyway. I can go to my sister's if things get bad, but I won't if I can help it. My neighbours will help — both sides. They're young, the husbands are big lads, they'll look after me. But what's Carl been up to this time, Jason? I'm worried about him."

He shakes his head. "You don't want to know, believe me, Julie. It's best I don't tell you. But I really need to find him, and quickly. Any idea where he's gone?"

She shrugs. "I wish I knew. But I don't know much about what he does anymore. You're the only one of his friends I know — I couldn't tell you who he sees or where he goes."

"Nor me. Did he say anything about where he was heading?"

"Nothing. I suppose you could try the tree surgeon. He works for them sometimes."

"Do you have their number?"

Julie rises from the table. "Now what were they called? I've got a card somewhere . . ."

She steps over to a small notice board by the back door where leaflets, notes and cards are pinned at random. She rifles through them, lifting scraps of paper to see what's underneath. "Got it! Here, take the number. It might be worth giving them a call. Though he doesn't seem to be doing much for them at the moment — more's the pity."

Jason types the name and number into his mobile. "It might help — thanks." He looks around. "Did he leave anything here when he stayed last week?"

"A backpack, I think. Go up to his room, have a look if you want."

"Thanks, Julie. It's worth a try."

He takes the stairs two by two and pushes open the door to Carl's old bedroom, the middle of three doors on the narrow landing. Everything's still there, as it was — posters of football teams, pop stars, racing cars. Some of them are battered, the corners torn, drooping from the wall. A few books on a shelf, a wardrobe filled with old clothes, a pile of T-shirts spilling out onto the floor. Old trainers under the bed. The same old Manchester United bedcover, rumpled, as if someone's been sitting there.

On the bed, a backpack. Jason holds it upside down, gives it a shake. An assortment of belongings falls out — sweet papers, matches, a small green packet of cigarette papers, some tobacco in a tin box. Evidence that Carl still smokes, though there was no sign of it when he stayed the night. He probably knew Alice would disapprove.

Jason rummages through a mess of receipts, bus tickets and coins that dropped from the front pocket. Nothing there gives him any clue. In the main compartment there's a woolly hat, a scarf, a half-empty bottle of water, a bus timetable and a few scraps of paper with pencil scribbles on. Some phone numbers, not local.

A larger piece of paper is folded into four. Intrigued, Jason opens it. It's a rough floor plan drawn in pencil, obviously without a ruler. There are two floors on the plan, the upper floor roughly sketched, indicating a number of bedrooms and en-suite bathrooms.

One of the rooms on the upper floor is highlighted in green, the word MONEY scrawled over it. It's the only room without a bathroom attached, and it contains a square box with five numbers on it.

Jason drops the paper as if it's on fire. What the hell? This is a plan of someone's house, with what looks suspiciously like a safe marked in an upstairs room. And if he's right, there, in black and white, is the code to open it.

Carl's planning to steal the money. That's how desperate he is.

Immediately Jason wishes he hadn't seen the scrap of paper. He doesn't want anything to do with it. But he can't un-see it now. For a moment he hesitates. Should he take the plan — or destroy it? But what difference would it make? He's only seen it once, for a few moments, and the details, including the numbers, are seared into his brain. He could probably redraw the plan quite accurately — and if he can, then surely Carl, who's intending to carry out a criminal act with the help of those pencil lines, could do it too.

He stuffs everything, including the plan, back into the backpack, wondering if he should back out now and leave Carl to his fate.

It's tempting — but he can't. He has to find him — and stop him.

CHAPTER 13

Alice

I'm about to pack up and go to bed when his message arrives. *Still no luck. Giving up, on my way back now xx*

It's not long before I hear his key in the lock. His face looks grey and drawn in the bright hallway, his smile not reaching his eyes. His jeans are stained, his trainers caked with mud. I stop him right there, enfolding him in my arms, saying nothing.

"God, I'm tired," he says into my shoulder. "I'm glad to be home."

"You're cold too." I take both his hands in mine and rub them. "Where are your gloves?"

"Left them here," he says, levering his shoes off with his toes. A hole in one sock reveals pale skin beneath. "I didn't expect to be wandering the rougher parts of West London tonight, to be honest."

I give him a sideways look.

He sighs, holding his hands out. "I know, I know."

"He doesn't deserve you." I leave it at that. He looks exhausted. It's not the right time to say more.

"Go on, take a shower, get warm. You look as if you need it."

"I tried everywhere I could think of — but nothing. I suppose I shouldn't be surprised. If a criminal gang's after him, he'll be properly holed up somewhere. I came back via the old route through the gardens, in case he'd hidden himself in a shed somewhere. That's how I got so grubby. At the bottom of those long gardens, you'd have no idea if someone was there or not."

"So, did you check ours as well?"

Jason freezes.

"Oh no, no . . ." Jason strides back out to the hall for his jacket and shoes. Within minutes he's unlocking the back door. I'm close behind, my heart thumping.

"Hold on, let's grab a torch — it's pitch black out there." He takes one from the hook behind the door and I follow, wondering what the neighbours will think if they happen to see us from their upstairs windows.

The garden has no lighting, and on a cloudy night like this the streetlamps struggle to illuminate more than a patch of pavement at the front of the house. A similar garden stretches beyond the footpath at the bottom to the back of a house on the parallel street, and on either side of the narrow lawn, trees and bushes create a corridor of darkness. As we approach the shed — an old-fashioned wooden hut housing the lawnmower and a few gardening tools — there's no warning light. I begin to think it's okay, we're being stupid to think he might be here. In the distance a police siren blares, fading away into the evening, leaving only the thrum of traffic interspersed with the growl of taxicabs. I shiver. There's a heavy dampness in the air, and I can't imagine what it would be like to spend the night out here in the freezing cold.

At the bottom of the garden, the shed crouches, half-hidden by hanging branches. There's no sign that anyone has been here, the key still in the lock as it always is, no sound penetrating the gloom.

"Carl?" Jason says, his voice resonating in the silence. "Are you in there?" The door creaks as he pushes it open. In the torchlight, strange shadows fall across the walls and

41

ceiling as he turns the beam from side to side. Old flow-er-pots are piled next to a rickety shelving unit where garden tools and bags of compost are piled in a mess. But there's no sign of Carl.

"He's not here." Jason turns to leave.

"Hang on a minute." I peer into a corner. "Jason, shine the torch over here. What's that?"

In a corner at the very back is what looks like a pile of blankets. In the glare of the torch I recognise our picnic blankets in a heap.

"It's nothing, just the picnic blankets," Jason says, his voice flat with disappointment.

"But wait — I didn't get them out. They were folded, in a bag." I look round — the bag is on the floor to one side. I pick up one of the blankets — a packet of Rizlas falls out. I bend to retrieve it. It's empty. I grab the torch from Jason's hand, sweeping the floor. A couple of spent matches and a crisp bag, also empty. I turn to Jason, who's staring at the flimsy box of cigarette papers.

"It's him, Jason!"

Slowly Jason takes the packet from my hand. "You're right," he says. "He was here."

I turn back to the heap of picnic blankets. I pick up the next one and gasp. In the centre is a deep, dark stain. It looks like blood.

CHAPTER 14

Alice

Darkness folds itself around the shed as we walk back to the house, shaking with cold — or shock.

"My God, Jason, what do you think happened?"

"I know as much as you do, I promise." He shakes his head. He looks even worse than he did before.

I close my eyes. "What are we getting into, Jason? He could have put us in danger by coming here."

"Probably why he didn't stay. He's not that stupid."

I snort. "But he is, though, isn't he? He's got himself into tons of shit in the past, many times. Now it looks like he's really gone and done it."

Jason looks exhausted and utterly miserable. "Do you want to call the police?"

"No! They won't do anything, they never do. Anyway, we still have nothing. Just a friend who's gone missing, but isn't really missing, and he's injured. He could have hurt himself climbing over the fence, for all we know. He reckons he's being chased by — somebody, we have no idea who — and he owes them money. The police will laugh at us."

"It's not enough for them to go on." Jason shivers. It's late and the heating's already been off for a couple of hours.

"Look, there's nothing more we can do today. Let's go and get warm."

"Please, tell me the whole story," I say as we climb into bed.

"I don't know the whole story."

"No, but — how much does he owe? And who to?"

"A hundred thousand quid." His words fall like stones onto hard ground.

My head swivels, my eyes widening. "What? Oh my word . . . a hundred thousand? You're kidding. Seriously — a *hundred grand*?"

"Nope, not kidding — I wish I was."

"But — who to? How come?"

"He called him Nick, but that's not his real name. Said he's into everything bad — drugs, girls, casinos, you name it. From a criminal family, with a gang to protect them. Couldn't be worse, really."

"But — a hundred thousand quid?" The size of it has me reeling. I'd thought maybe ten, twenty — but this? It doesn't bear thinking about. "What the hell was he doing? Now I know why he's so scared. But — it was a property deal, right? Is that what it's all about?"

"Yes, some scheme in the Caribbean, believe it or not."

A too-good-to-be-true property deal in the Caribbean. That figures. "Can't he get the money back from the developer — or take it to court?"

Jason shakes his head, frowning. "It's useless. The guy's gone bankrupt. He's legged it. There's no way to get it back."

It takes me a few minutes to clear my head. I can't imagine ever being in debt for that kind of money — except for a mortgage, I suppose, but that seems different somehow. A mortgage is agreed by two parties, and you only take one on if you can afford the repayments — or at least, that's what sensible people do. That's the only kind of debt I've ever contemplated. Otherwise, I hate owing more than a few pounds on a credit card, and even then, I pay the balance off every month. Jason's the same. Neither of us takes risks when it comes to money.

"I suppose . . ." I hesitate.

"What?"

"If he went to the police . . ."

"You — suggesting the police? That's a first."

"I know. But maybe he can get some kind of protection."

"I doubt it. He'll get locked up for not paying his debts, and this guy Nick will still get to him. He won't be safe in prison, not with a gang like that — wherever he's sent, he'll be vulnerable. He'll end up in a wheelchair . . . or dead."

My stomach lurches.

"When I said he's in serious shit, I meant it," Jason says. "He can't get a loan for more than a grand or two, and even then only from one of those dodgy operations that rips you off so you can never pay them back. He's got no job, no references, no house to sell, no savings."

"Is there a deadline? I mean, perhaps we could get it extended . . ."

"He's way past the deadline. The bad guys are out to get him. Even if he's able to get some of the money now, I doubt he'd get away without a terrible beating, or worse."

"But then they'd never get their money."

"That's what I said. But he's not convinced."

"Christ. I almost feel sorry for him." I really do, for the first time. He's reckless, and stupid — but he doesn't deserve that.

Jason looks shocked. "You do?"

"Is there nobody in his family that can help? His mum? Some distant uncle, or cousin — anyone?"

Jason grimaces. "He can't ask his mum. She has no money — she'd have to sell the house. She'd be homeless and he couldn't live with that. He's adamant he won't go that route — and I'm not going to encourage him to. There's no other family."

"What happened to his dad?"

"Dead end, I'm afraid. He took off when Carl was little. He's never known him. In school he'd just say he didn't have a dad. He made it clear that was the end of the conversation, and nobody pushed him."

"Doesn't he have any ideas of his own? He must be able to find at least some of the money, surely?" I can't believe he's utterly helpless, despite all the evidence.

"I'm afraid not. He's out of ideas."

"Well, he'll have to leave the country," I say. "That's all there is for it."

"He'll have to go a long, long way. And stay there. God, Alice, I wish I knew where he was. Then at least I can try to help him."

"You've always tried to protect him, Jason. Even when he let you down all the time."

Jason nods. "I know. More fool me."

I wonder if this is the right time, but we're not sleepy, and I might as well ask. "Did something happen when you were younger? To make you feel that you owed him? I've always wondered, and Dawn hinted at it the other day. It made me curious again."

CHAPTER 15

Jason

It had been raining for days and the ground was sodden, the mud sticking to the soles of their trainers as they walked. They'd been hanging about in the park near home, the three of them — Carl, Jason and Patrick, a lad from school who'd joined them for a sneaky cigarette. But the park had little to offer — a few bushes to hide behind, a single tree they sometimes climbed and sat in, throwing twigs at kids down below. But for teenage boys, not much to keep them occupied, and they were bored. Not one of them wanted to go back home, where they'd be in trouble for the mud on their shoes, for the homework waiting to be done.

It was Carl's idea to take the trip, of course. They hung about the station for a while, joshing each other, pretending to push one another towards the line. At one point, after a particularly evil shove from Carl, Jason almost fell under the wheels of an approaching train. He responded angrily and the two of them ended up wrestling on the platform until a passenger complained. The station master appeared, gave them a severe roasting, and made them sit on a bench until their train came. In the carriage, Carl and Jason carried on muttering at each other, elbowing and pushing, pulling at each other's clothes. Jason kicked Carl hard on the shin, making him yell with pain. They sat separately for the rest of the journey.

It hadn't been raining when they left. It started to drizzle while they were on the train, but as they approached Shott's Hill it began to come down in great soaking bucketfuls, like someone was throwing water bombs from the roofs of the houses around them. Their clothes were useless — jeans, trainers and hoodies soaked up the water like sponges, hanging heavy on their thin frames. When they got to the rocky waterfall, Carl said: "Let's climb it. We're soaked already — what's the difference?"

Blinking through fat droplets on their eyelashes, the other boys looked up at the steep incline, where the water gushed and splashed across shining rocks. They were cold and miserable. Still smarting from Carl's behaviour at the station, Jason would rather have turned back, but didn't want to be the one to say it. Patrick shrugged and nodded his head, so Jason did the same. Carl was hard to argue with, and the climb didn't look too bad. Without the rain it would have been fun. They followed Carl's lead.

It was already getting dark, and they had no torch between them. Carl pulled out his mobile, using its light to lead the way, Patrick following close behind. As Jason watched from below, the two of them reached the halfway point, a flat ledge not too far up. There was a clear path to that point, zig-zagging upwards through the rocks, barely visible in the failing light.

From below it looked slippery and treacherous. As Jason hesitated at the bottom, blinking through the rain, Carl shouted: "Come on, Jason, don't be a wimp, it's easy. You can't pull out now, we're not coming back down."

Jason had very little choice if he didn't want to be left to find his own way back. "Okay, I'm coming," he said. "Shine the light on the path for me, will you?"

"Don't go that way," Carl shouted back. "There's a quicker way, look, over here."

Jason lost sight of the two boys for a moment as they moved to the other side of the ledge. When they reappeared, they were crouching on a large overhanging rock. Carl shone the light as Jason began the climb. It wasn't difficult to get close to where the two boys waited — until he reached the very last part. There everything glistened in the bright torchlight. Water streamed across the overhanging rock, splashing onto Jason's face as he tried to make out how to climb over.

"Here, take my hand," Carl shouted, crouching close to the edge. He reached down, but Jason was blinded by the mini-waterfall. He stretched one arm towards Carl, his feet scrabbling. He was almost there, he'd got a foothold — but something was wrong. His hand grasped thin air and water. For a moment he managed to keep his balance, but then — his body teetered backwards, his sodden trainers sliding away from underneath him.

He was dimly aware of his head cracking against a rock before everything went dark.

* * *

"I was swept away — the river was running so fast. Patrick called for help but Carl ran after me as I was dragged down the river. He jumped in and hauled me out. Then he carried me — I don't know how he did it — along the road until a car pulled over and picked us up. I would have drowned if he hadn't saved me. We were taken to hospital: I had a bad head wound and was unconscious and Carl was suffering from exhaustion."

"Wow. That was brave. Though it was his idea in the first place."

"He's not entirely to blame. We went along with it. It was pretty stupid."

So that's why Jason is so loyal to him. Carl saved his life. It's a good enough reason. It says a lot for Jason that he feels the weight of the debt after all this time.

But it doesn't say much for Carl, still taking advantage.

"You don't need to carry that debt for ever, you know. Carl hasn't exactly been a great friend to you."

"I know." Jason sighs. "I suppose it became a habit. Carl had a hold over me at school and I've never really broken free."

"It's not right, you know. You've been a good friend to him when he didn't deserve it. You don't need to support him anymore."

There's a long pause. Then Jason says softly: "I'm not your dad, you know, Alice."

I bite my lip. "I'm sorry. Of course you're not." I give him a reassuring squeeze. But deep down, I'm not so sure. My dad was easily led, too. To say the least.

"But why didn't you tell me? I might have liked Carl better if I'd known."

"There's no mystery about it. I suppose there were things I did when I was a kid that I'm not proud of. That was the worst of them. It was terrible for my parents — they thought I was going to die. I felt so bad for them. It was a stupid adventure gone badly wrong, and they bore the brunt of it. I was ashamed I got dragged into it."

"They must have been so grateful to Carl."

"They were. The problem is he makes sure I never forget about it. I changed after that day, but I don't think he did, not a bit. He carried on in his usual mad, irresponsible way. To be honest, I was relieved when he moved away. I hoped he wouldn't come back."

"Well, he's certainly back," I say drily.

CHAPTER 16

Jason

Jason's brain is buzzing; sleep is beyond reach. He checks the time on his mobile, creeps downstairs. Wrapping himself in a blanket, he opens his laptop. There must be a way out of Carl's mess. He lists the options, trying to think clearly through a fog of exhaustion.

But, too soon, he's out of ideas. He runs his fingers through his hair, gazing at what he's written, forcing his mind to keep thinking. But the whole thing seems hopeless — Carl doesn't have a chance.

He's about to go back to bed when he's startled by his mobile. Unknown number: it can only be Carl.

"Jason, it's me."

"Carl. Where are you — are you okay? We found blood . . ."

"I'm outside. Are you up? I saw a light—"

"Hold on, I'm coming." Jason drops his phone in his haste to get to the front door.

Carl makes a sorry figure, thin and stooped, a grubby hood over his head. When he looks up, it's clear his nose is broken; it's misshapen, almost disappearing amid the purple swelling on his cheeks. His eyes are barely visible and there's a nasty cut on his forehead. He glances behind him.

"Shit, Carl, you look terrible."

"Thanks." He steps inside.

"Alice is asleep. Come into the kitchen. I'll get you something to eat."

Soon Carl has a hot cup of tea in his hand and a sandwich in front of him.

"What happened — the same guy?"

"Yeah, but this is nothing compared with what they'd like to do to me." He shrugs. His fingers run down his battered nose. "It looks worse than it is."

"Chasing the money?"

"Yeah, and it'll be worse next time."

"How did you manage to get away this time? Did you lose another jacket?"

Carl snorts. "Funny." His eyes slide away. "It doesn't matter. They won't let me off next time — they made that crystal clear."

"At least let me clean up that cut on your forehead."

It's deep, and it's still oozing. Jason soaks a cloth with warm water and bathes it as best he can, patching it up with a plaster. "That'll have to do for the moment. You really should see a doctor, though — it looks like it needs stitching."

"It'll be okay. Listen, Jason, I've found a way out of this."

"You have?"

"Yes. But I need your help." Carl is suddenly animated, his eyes fixed on Jason. "I have a plan."

The familiar twist in his gut reminds Jason of his teenage years. He has a horrible suspicion about this plan. "Why don't I feel excited about this?"

Carl's face is a ruin of bruises and cuts, the kitchen light casting grey shadows over the purple patches. He has to lift his chin to look at Jason. His eyes are tiny slits, the swollen, angry flesh around them almost obscuring them. "Listen, mate, this is serious. I wouldn't ask if it wasn't, believe me."

"Just tell me."

"Okay." Carl leans forward over the table, moving his drink out of the way. "I know where I can get the money. It'll be tricky, but I know how to get hold of it — the whole lot, and more. It's foolproof."

Jason closes his eyes. *Oh God. This is bad.* "Christ. Don't tell me you're planning to nick the money. Please don't tell me that."

"Yeah, but — no, wait—"

Jason stops him with a hand. "Don't even think of telling me if it's illegal."

Carl makes a calming gesture, his eyes pleading.

"Hear me out, Jason, please."

"Honestly, Carl. I'm not in that game, not me. Not ever."

"I know, I know. But this is perfect — I promise. He won't involve the police. And he won't know it's us."

Us? The word resonates around Jason's head like a ghostly echo. He wants to say: *Stop right there, Carl — there is no "us".*

Instead, he says: "Who — who's 'he'?"

"You remember I said I got some work on a building site? Yeah, well a few years ago, I did a lot of work for this one guy — Needham, his name is — Graham Needham. He did all these smart mansions, swanky places — footballers' houses, know what I mean? Bought the land cheap with some old bungalow on it, usually after some old person died, and transformed it. Top quality, you know? Marble floors, smart fittings, swimming pools, state-of-the-art security, all that. Property was booming and he made an absolute killing. All of it in cash — he insisted on being paid in ready money. It was a win-win. He avoided the taxman, his clients avoided VAT. He paid just enough to keep the Revenue off his back, kept the rest. He was as bent as bent could be, I tell you."

"Is he going to lend you the money, then?" Jason says, drily.

"Just hear me out, will you? Me and him, we became drinking mates. Mates, you know. He gave me work, I kept my mouth shut about what I knew. Then, well, I let him down once or twice." Carl drops his eyes.

53

"Let him down?" He doesn't know why he's asking. He knows exactly what Carl means.

"Forgot to turn up for a job, nicked some things that were lying around, nothing special, just some bits and bobs."

Jason shakes his head. This is familiar territory.

"He dropped me. Yelled at me not to bother him anymore. Threatened to tell the police. I was pretty sure he wouldn't do anything — I knew too much about him. He sacked me, and that was that. But I stayed friends with the lads, went drinking with them sometimes. Then he booted one of them, too, his security guy, bloke called Chris. He's the one who used to put in all these fancy security systems in the big posh houses — complicated electronics linking to mobile apps and all."

"Sounds like this Needham fellow falls out with a lot of his staff."

"Yeah, well, it's a bit of both really. I deserved what I got — Chris probably did too."

"So . . ."

"Anyway, we were out one night shortly after Chris got the old heave-ho. He got very drunk. He'd been on good money — needed it, with a wife and four kids. He was pretty cut up that he'd lost his job. Kept on saying he'd get Graham back one day, he had enough on him to go to the police, that sort of thing. Turns out Chris installed a safe in Graham's house — he told me all about it, even the code. I wrote it on my hand when he wasn't looking. Graham must be well over seventy now, lives on his own. His wife and kids left him years ago — he never sees them. Anyway, it was upstairs, in one of the smaller bedrooms."

"What did he keep in there, then?" But he knows the answer already. The sketchy plan, the word written in capital letters.

"Graham let it slip." Carl stops, gazing at Jason with a strange smile on his face. "The money, Jason. Tens of thousands in cash, maybe hundreds, even. A fortune, sitting there waiting for us to rescue it."

CHAPTER 17

Jason

He can't help it — his mouth falls open. For a moment, he's speechless.

It's not so much that Carl thinks he can pull it off, a burglary of that magnitude. It's that he's thinking, even for one second, that Jason's going to help him.

He snaps his jaw shut. "Oh no. No, no, no, Carl. What the fuck do you mean, *rescue it?* This isn't some abused cat you're talking about." Jason lowers his voice with an effort. There's no way he wants Alice to wake up and get embroiled in this. "What you're suggesting to me, even after I've made it absolutely clear I'm not getting involved in anything illegal, is . . . *huge*. And criminal, and probably impossible. You're out of your mind." He stands, expecting Carl to follow him. "You can sleep on the sofa, but you need to leave when it gets light."

But Carl stays put. "No, wait, just let me explain. Two minutes. Sit down — please — listen for two minutes — that's all. If you're not interested, we'll forget all about it. Please, Jason." The words pour out of his misshapen mouth.

Jason has run out of the energy to stop him. "Okay. Two minutes — but I'm not going to change my mind." He sits.

"Okay. Graham's retired now — but he owes a huge amount to the Revenue. He can't go to the police, can he, they'd be all over him like a rash. And Chris was out of his head. He doesn't even remember he told me. The security in the house hasn't been updated for years — Graham's too tight. Nobody else knows about the money. It's a slam dunk."

A slam dunk? He can't believe his ears. Carl has lost the plot, seriously.

"No, Carl. What do you think I am? I've never even nicked so much as a snack bar, let alone carried out a full-scale burglary! And if you think I'm going to prison for you, you've got another think coming."

"I can't do it on my own — it needs two people. You have to help me, Jason."

Jason's stunned. Carl hasn't heard a word he has said. He really is a piece of work. He should have refused to let him in. He should have known this was coming. Fury bubbles in his chest, threatening to explode.

"Right, that's your two minutes up. The answer's still no, and it's not going to change. I'm not doing it. Come on, Carl. I'll find you a blanket."

But Carl stays put. He looks to one side and pauses, as if deciding on something.

"The thing is, mate, you're involved already."

It's like a punch in the stomach. "What? What do you mean, I'm involved?"

Carl's eyes flick from one side to the other. His voice drops. "The bad guys — they know about you. I told them you're going to help me get the money. That's why they let me go."

CHAPTER 18

Jason

"You've told them what?" Anger, horror and disbelief flow through him in turn.

Carl drops his head. "They think we were together in that property deal—"

"What? What do you mean, together? How — why would they think that?"

"They were going to kill me — I had to say something!"

"But you put them on to me? Why the fuck would you do that? You know I haven't got any money!"

Carl hangs his head. "I'm sorry, Jason."

"Sorry doesn't do it, Carl. So you landed me in it? You're supposed to look out for your friends — not put them in danger!"

"I–I was trying to pacify them — thinking on my feet."

This is terrible — worse than he could possibly have imagined. He leans forward, locking his eyes onto Carl's, one finger pointing. When he realises, he folds his fist around the finger and puts it behind his back, so he can't be tempted to use it. "Carl, I swear, if I was a different man, I'd kill you myself." It's a huge effort to control his anger. "I suppose you gave them my name and address, too . . . you'd have given them my bank details, my pension, put them in touch with my mortgage company, given half a chance. Do you care about anyone else but yourself, Carl? Do you?"

Carl flinches. His eyes open wide. A pleading look flashes across his face. "Jason, I—"

"Don't you play the innocent with me! You've never taken any responsibility for yourself. Well now you've got no choice. You're unbelievable." For the first time in his life, he's ready to give up on Carl.

"I know, I know. I'm sorry—"

"Don't bother to apologise. I don't believe anything you say."

A look of desperation crosses Carl's face. His voice is like rough gravel. "Believe this, Jason. If I don't get them their money, they'll kill me. And then they'll come for you. And Alice — and your mum, as well as mine. These guys never give up."

Jason stares at Carl. In this moment, he hates him. But he's involved, whether he likes it or not, and his family is in real danger. He feels trapped, like he's sinking in quicksand.

"But, Jason, there is another way — there is."

Not this again. "What, your crazy, idiotic burglary? Forget it. Get it out of your thick head. Do you want to spend the next decade in prison? Because that's what will happen if you try something like that."

"You don't understand. Graham won't go to the police, he can't. It's a shoo-in. No, it really is—"

Jason jumps up, stiff with anger. "I'm not listening, Carl. Don't you get it? I'm not interested. I can't help you, you'll have to sort out your own shit for once." He turns to go.

"Wait, Jason — wait!" Carl's out of his chair, grasping Jason by the sleeve. Jason shakes him off, but not before he notices the tears in Carl's eyes. Despite himself, he hesitates.

"I'll do it myself." Carl talks fast. "I'll get some climbing gear from the tree surgeons, I know where they keep it.

That'll get me over the wall and up to the first floor, no problem. I've watched the house, I know what Graham's routine is. He goes to the pub around six every evening. When he gets in, he drinks himself stupid and sleeps on the sofa until the early hours. Then he locks up, puts the alarm on and staggers upstairs to bed. If we — if I get in and out while he's still downstairs, I don't need to bother disabling the main alarm because it won't be set. I know where the safe is — it's in a room upstairs. As long as I can get into that room, I can get the money. I've got the code for the safe."

Jason pictures the rough drawing of the house, the room marked *MONEY*, the scribbled numbers. "You're completely mad. Why are you telling me this if you don't need me? I don't want to know . . ."

"But I do need you — to drive me there. I can't exactly walk to his house with the gear over my shoulder now, can I? And walk back out with a bag full of notes?"

"Oh, no." He shakes his head in disbelief. "I'm not doing it. You're nuts." He goes for the door — but Carl's hand is on his arm again, pulling him back.

"C'mon, Jason. I'm not asking much, am I? If we — I — get caught, you'll be in the clear. I'll take the rap, I promise."

"Don't be daft, Carl. I'd still be an accessory. I told you from the beginning, I can't help you. You can try as hard as you like to push me into a guilt trip but I'm not doing it. No, Carl."

Anger gives Jason the strength to wrestle the hand from his arm and turn away.

"I'm going to bed." Jason's voice cracks with pent-up anger. "Stay on the sofa if you want, but get out before morning. Don't contact me again."

CHAPTER 19

Alice

I watch Jason's haggard face as he pushes his breakfast away. I felt his absence in the night, my hand searching for him on cold sheets. It was a long time before he slipped back under the duvet. In the meantime, I dozed, but I feel wrung out this morning.

"Are you okay?"

He looks as if he's about to cry. "No, not really." He pushes his fingers through his hair in a gesture of hopelessness.

I put my hand over his. It's cold, and he doesn't move in response. "Listen, I know you're worried about Carl. But what can you do? Even if he tries to contact you, he could be putting you — us — in danger."

But Jason looks so forlorn. His natural instinct is to help, and this time he can't. "I know your heart wants to save him, but your head knows you can't. It's awful but he's got to work this one out for himself."

"I know. You're right, of course. But I can't help imagining what the consequences might be. And what it might do to Julie."

"Yes, but he's not your responsibility, Jason, and nor is she."

"I know." Jason nods, but I can see his mind's still working on it. "I'd better get to work." He gives me a kiss on the cheek and is gone.

A few minutes later I'm ready to go too when the doorbell rings. Thinking he's forgotten his keys, I fling the door open.

But it's not Jason. It's a thick-set, balding man in jeans and an ill-fitting jacket. I step back, startled.

"Ah, sorry to bother you," he says, looking me up and down with a sneer. "Do you live here?"

It's a strange question, and I'm instantly suspicious. "Yes, why?"

"Is your husband in?"

My hackles rise. I step forward, my hand on the door, ready to slam it shut. "Who wants to know?"

"Apologies. I was looking for . . . er, Mr Jones."

"Well, he doesn't live here. You've got the wrong house." I start to close the door, but his hand is on it, pushing back. I stand my ground, though I'm quaking inside. I'm vulnerable, and if he decides to come in, I'm not sure I can stop him.

"Any idea where he might live?"

"Not a clue."

He smiles. More like a leer. "No worries. Sorry to disturb." He's heading for the gate as I close the front door, my legs shaking with relief.

There's something very wrong here. Nobody rings on a random front door like that. I run up the stairs to see where he goes.

From the bedroom window, I spot him easily. He hasn't gone far. He's across the road, talking to the postman. The postman nods and points at our house. As they look up, I pull back from the window, my heart racing.

It's them. They know where we live.

My fingers shake as I hold my phone. "Jason, someone was here."

"What do you mean, someone?"

"I thought you'd come back for something, but it was — well, I don't know who it was, but he asked if anyone else lived here and then he went and spoke to the postman. They were definitely talking about our house."

"What did he look like?"

"Bald, thick-set. He asked for Mr Jones, but it was obvious he'd just conjured that up as a reason for being here. Are we in danger, Jason?"

Jason hesitates for a moment. "Look, I don't know, but it sounds strange. Get a taxi to work, and I'll pick you up later. We'll talk about it tonight."

"I'm spooked by all this, Jason. You've got to do something."

"I'm trying, believe me."

"You have to get rid of Carl. I'm beginning to get really scared."

CHAPTER 20

Alice

I notice the dark smudges beneath Dawn's eyes, the lines etched on her forehead.

"You look tired, Dawn. Let me help." I take a bag from her.

"Shopping always gives me a headache," she says. "Probably that dreadful lighting at the supermarket. But nothing to worry about. Sit down, both of you, and chat to me while I cook. Jason, tell me about Carl. What's he up to now?"

"You don't want to know, Mum."

"That bad, eh?" She turns concerned eyes to him.

I throw Jason a warning look. We don't want to worry Dawn with Carl's antics. He's got everyone else running around after him — Dawn doesn't need to waste her energy on him, too.

Jason gives me a small nod. "He'll work something out, I'm sure," he says. "He always seems to find a way to dodge the bullet."

"Let's hope his luck doesn't run out this time, then," Dawn says. "How's Julie?"

"She's pretty worried about him."

"I'm not surprised, I'd worry, if I was his mum. Thank goodness I'm not." Dawn pats Jason on the leg. "Wouldn't change my Jason for the world."

"Hasn't he spoken to her?" I'm angry enough with Carl. For him to leave his mum guessing is pretty shabby, in my book.

"Nope. He hasn't been in touch with her, not even a text to say he's okay."

What I want to say is *He's a bastard, through and through. Why are you bothering with him?* But I resist, though I can't help my frustration breaking through. "He's not okay, though, is he? This time, he's really gone and done it."

Jason flashes me a warning look.

"What's he done?" Dawn's eyes flick between us.

"Nothing you need to know about, Mum. He's got himself into another scrape. A bit more of a grown-up scrape than usual, that's all."

"Well, don't get dragged into it, will you, Jason — please?"

"It's fine, Mum, please don't worry. I won't do anything stupid."

Dawn gives him a nod, reassured. But he won't make eye contact with me.

There's something he's not telling me, I'm sure of it.

64

CHAPTER 21

Jason

His mobile rings. Number unknown. Normally he wouldn't bother to answer, especially at work. But with all that's happening, he can't ignore it. Cursing under his breath, he taps the green telephone icon.

"Hello?"

"This is DS Bennett from Acton Police. This number came up on a mobile phone we're investigating. Can I ask who I'm speaking to?" The voice is male, strident. Alarms screech in Jason's head, his chest tightens.

"Jason — Jason Green."

"Let me explain. We were called out to an incident last night — early this morning. A man is in hospital. He's in an induced coma with a severe head injury. We haven't been able to identify him — he had no belongings with him, only this phone. With your number on."

Jesus Christ, Carl, what have you done? The fist behind his ribs tightens its grip. His breath comes in short, sharp gasps. He forces himself to breathe normally.

What should he tell the police?

"R-really?" The word escapes as a strangled squeak.

"Do you have any idea who this might be, and why your number is the only one saved on his mobile?"

He plays for time, speaking slowly while his mind rushes on. He's glad the police officer doesn't know him, because his voice no longer sounds like his own. "I'm — I'm not sure. Can you tell me anything about him? What does he look like?"

"Youngish, slim, Caucasian, dark hair. Wearing jeans and a hoodie, piercings in his left ear. A tattoo of a rose on his right arm. Anybody come to mind?"

That's Carl. Jason's heart is somewhere down by his feet, his hands shaking, a cold sweat breaking out on his temples.

"That's Carl Jackson. He's a friend. What happened?"

"He was found slumped behind some bins in an empty car park. A shift worker came across him in the early hours. Not far from where you live, actually. He was lucky to be found when he was — he was in a bad way. When did you see him last?"

Don't say too much. Stay calm. "He — he stayed over last night. But he didn't say where he was going. Which hospital is he in?"

"I'll tell you, but you can't see him yet. Unless you're family." He spells out the name of a nearby hospital. "Do you know of any relatives we can get in touch with?"

"Yes, I know his mum, she lives near here." He finds Julie's contact details, reads the number out. His fingers tremble. "But — what happened to him? Will he be okay?"

"Looks like he's been badly beaten up. He's unconscious, possibly concussed. It'll be a while before we know the details — most likely not before he wakes up. That's if he remembers anything."

"That's terrible."

"Do you know of any reason he might be in trouble?"

"I — er, sorry, no," he stammers. "Sorry, I — it's the shock . . ."

"I understand, sir." From his tone, the officer understands only too well. Jason is prevaricating. He knows something. He curses himself for being so readable.

"I wonder if you could come into the station to give us a statement. You might be able to help us with our enquiries."

"Okay. Wh — when?" He almost chokes on the word. He's always been a terrible liar. Even in that short phone call he's given himself away. If he goes into the police station, he's not sure he can stand up to their questioning.

But if he's got to go in, at least it gives him some time to organise his thoughts.

"Thank you. As soon as you can, please. Ask for me — DS Bennett."

Jason's mind whirs as he cuts the call. He doesn't know what to do next. Should he contact Julie? She's probably speaking to the police officer right now.

The idea of a police interview is terrifying. He can't tell them about the loan — that would only land Carl in trouble. He certainly can't tell them about the plan to steal it. But it will be on his mind the whole time. How will he manage to get through an interview if he's shaking with nerves at the very thought of it?

If he's going to persuade the police he knows nothing, he's going to have to put on one hell of a performance.

CHAPTER 22

Jason

Carl out of intensive care and conscious.

Jason breathes a little easier. Julie's next text has the opposite effect. *Carl asking for you urgently. Can you come?*

A sense of foreboding creeps over Jason, like a shadow blocking out the sun. This can only be trouble. If he was terrified before, Carl must be beside himself now. He needs no further proof that Carl's life's in danger.

I'll come ASAP. Hope you're okay.

Thanks — he's very scared. Hope you can help him.

I'll do my best.

As he walks to his car, the realisation comes over him that even while Carl's lying in hospital, the threat hasn't gone away. If the gang finds out he's survived, they could be waiting for their chance to finish him off. They could also be waiting for Jason to visit. He'll have to be careful, alert to danger.

This is how it's going to be, for all of them, until the debt is paid. It's a horrible realisation.

The hospital foyer is frenetic. It's like a different world, everything happening at once, dramas in progress all over the place. Jason surveys the room, his stress levels rising. A couple carrying a child run past him, startling him. They jump the queue to get attention. A nurse leaves the desk and ushers them through some swing doors to one side. An ambulance draws up outside, a trolley is unloaded. It rumbles past Jason, guided by ambulance crew. They push it through the double doors and on down the main corridor, their shoes squeaking on the shiny floor. People sit on rows of plastic chairs, some with takeaway cups in their hands, some nursing injuries, their faces pale. Children play on the grey linoleum, their mothers watching over them with tired eyes, while a drunk shouts and guffaws to himself in a corner.

Jason waits in line, intimidated by the noise, the bright lights, the never-ending movement. He watches the entrance doors, just in case. They swish every few seconds as people come and go, and outside there's a constant stream of head-lights as ambulances and cars disgorge their passengers and move on. But nobody seems interested in him.

At the desk he asks for Carl, saying he's his brother. Now he's here, he must see him, even if he has to lie to do it. The receptionist, a uniformed woman whose eyes flit around the room as she speaks, gives him directions without a question. Fifth floor, ward on the right. He hurries towards the lift, following a line of yellow footprints painted on the floor, keeping an eye on the stretch of corridor behind him.

A slim figure lies in a bed by the window, its head resting on a pile of pillows. Something about the profile is familiar. But when Jason approaches the head turns, stopping him in his tracks. One eye is buried in purple, swollen flesh. Most of the face is swathed in bandages, as are both hands. A flimsy hospital gown reveals dressings on one shoulder and there's a dark smear of blood on the pale skin of his neck.

"Carl?"

The figure tenses, its chin lifting as the single eye searches through bruised flesh. The damaged mouth moves. "Jason." It's almost a whisper.

Jason draws up a chair, trying to keep the shock from his face. He's never seen anything like it. There's not much skin to be seen, but what he can see is swollen beyond recognition, splashed with a rainbow of weals. It's as if a toddler has taken a paintbrush to Carl's body.

"My God, Carl. What the hell happened?"

Carl tries to push himself up onto the pillows, his bandaged hands pressing down on either side of his hips, but he stops with a cry of pain.

"Here, don't try to move." He settles Carl back against the pillows. "Stay where you are. Do you want some water?"

He holds the beaker as the swollen lips close around the straw. Carl gulps once, twice, then lies back with a grimace.

He signals for Jason to lean forward, his eye swivelling around the ward. Jason glances over his shoulder. "There's nobody here, Carl, you're safe."

A bandaged hand grabs his jumper with surprising strength, pulling him close.

"I'm not safe here — not anywhere. You — you've got to — get me out of here," Carl whispers. Close up, Jason can see a bloodstained gap where Carl's front tooth should be. The effect is both comical and ghastly.

He removes Carl's hand, laying it back down on the sheet. "No way, mate. Look at you, you can barely move. You need to rest, get better. Looks like you've got more than a few broken bones."

Carl's single eye blazes. "No, listen — they tried to kill me."

"And they'll try to kill you again if you leave. You're safer in here."

"I'm a bloody sitting duck."

Jason looks around. The whole floor seems deserted. Nobody suspicious watching them. In fact, no one there at all. The silence makes him feel even more uncomfortable. "Didn't the police send anyone to guard you?"

The wounded lips curl. He shakes his head slowly. "No chance of that. Listen — we have to get the money, my way. You know what I'm talking about. You have to help me."

Jason flinches. "Carl, I told you—"

"No, I'm telling you, it's the only way." Each word seems painful, the effort exhausting. The single eye closes for a moment.

"It may be, but you can't go anywhere like this. We'll talk about it when you're better, okay?" He doesn't want to think about Carl's plan.

The eye opens. It's like a laser beam, pinning Jason into his seat. "I gotta get out."

"Carl, listen to me. You can't leave. Out there, where are you going to go? How will you get better? Here, you've got a bed, food, someone looking out for you. Anyway, you look gruesome — hardly recognisable. No one's going to come near you." It's a feeble attempt at a joke.

Carl grimaces again, the battered eye closing.

"Listen, I'll have a word with the nurses, tell them you're worried someone's after you, get them to keep a special eye on you. I'll come as often as I can. No, I won't try and get you out early—" Carl is shaking his head. "You have to get well first. It'll be even harder for you to defend yourself if you discharge yourself now. You need proper care and here's the best place."

There's a long pause before Carl turns his ruined face to Jason. "They'll come for you next," he croaks.

CHAPTER 23

Jason

Driving to the police station, Jason bites the inside of his cheek until it bleeds, the metallic taste giving him an odd sense of relief. Seeing Carl, the state he's in, has shaken him to the core. He must stop, try to relax, or he'll give himself away for sure.

He's relieved to find it's not DS Bennett taking his statement, but a junior officer. She's small and neat, her hair pulled back into a bun. She looks about twenty. She asks only a few questions, writing everything down carefully, interrupting only to clarify a point. He's able to act the innocent. Which of course he is, he reminds himself — it's just that he's not revealing everything.

After what seems like a very long time, she leans back in her seat. "That's it, I have no more questions for you today. Is there anything else you want to tell me about Mr Jackson, or what's happened to him?"

"N-no, that's all I know, I'm afraid. But I was wondering—"

"Yes?"

"Given we — you — have no idea who's responsible for this, and why they attacked him, is he still in danger? I mean, if they thought they'd killed him — what happens when they find out he's alive?"

She seems taken aback, so he pushes home the suggestion. "Sounds like they almost did kill him, to me."

She nods. "Indeed. The doctor said if he hadn't been found when he was, he might not have made it through the night. I'll talk to my superior officer." She stands, pushing her chair back under the table.

"Thank you. Will you put a guard on his room?"

"I'll have a word." She opens the door and gestures for him to go ahead.

"Thanks. It would be reassuring to know someone's keeping an eye out."

"And you're sure you have no idea who might have done this?"

He keeps his gaze steady. "I have absolutely no idea."

CHAPTER 24

Alice

"You've known since this morning?" I sink into a chair. "Oh, Jason, why didn't you call me? That's terrible — poor Carl. Poor Julie!"

Jason leans against the kitchen worktop, as if too weary to stand up. "Honestly, I didn't have time to call you. By the time I'd gone to the hospital and given my statement to the police, I really needed to get back to work. They were good about it, but I felt bad. I worked like crazy this afternoon to catch up. Luckily, I managed to get most of it under my belt by the time I left. I'm whacked."

"What did the police say? Did you tell them he owes money?"

He shakes his head. "They didn't ask."

I open my mouth but close it again. It's not up to me what Jason decides to tell the police.

"You said yourself, you don't want me to get involved," he continues. "I don't know who this guy 'Nick' is — I know nothing about him or his family. What's the point in telling them? It'll only get Carl into trouble."

He's right — if the police are to be involved, it's Carl's decision, not Jason's. And I want nothing to do with the cops.

I shake my head, still shocked. "I'm so sorry. This is terrible."

"It's awful, and I'm worried he's still in danger. I suggested they might want to put a copper on guard outside his room, in case the heavies try to finish him off. I don't know if they will, though."

I stand, putting my arms around Jason, feeling his solid warmth against my chest. But I can feel the tension in his body. I release him and he turns away, gazing over the garden with unseeing eyes.

"But surely they wouldn't want him dead?" I say. "How would they get their money then? At least while he's alive there's a chance. Even if he has to steal it."

Jason gives me a strange look. "He's not a criminal, Alice."

Guilt stabs at me, for even thinking it. "No, I know. Sorry. I'm clutching at straws. But, Jason—"

"I know — neither was your dad. Until he was. But, you know, underneath all the swagger, Carl is quite naive. He's never been in serious trouble before. He has no idea how to handle these guys. It's a completely different world. If he tries thieving to get the money, he could end up in prison, and in there, things could get much worse . . ."

I daren't think of the things that might happen to someone like Carl, in prison with hardened criminals. But I know enough to be certain that he would suffer — badly. And he might not survive the experience. Even if he managed to serve the term, his life would never be the same again.

A horrible thought occurs to me. These people, the gang — whoever they are — have just beaten Carl to within an inch of his life. They probably think they've killed him. But that won't be the end of it, if Carl's right about this guy Nick. "Jason, you don't think—"

"What?"

"I'm just thinking — if they can't get what they want from Carl, what will they do next? Is Julie in danger?" I hesitate. "Are we?"

There's a long pause, but Jason doesn't answer. "Jason?"

I'm beginning to feel panicky now. "Surely they can't expect us to have that kind of money? And if we did, why would they think we'd give it to Carl?"

He hangs his head. "I'm so sorry, Alice." His voice is gruff, emotional.

"What do you mean — why are you sorry?"

He can't meet my eyes.

"What?" My scalp tingles. I feel the blood rush to my face. "You mean they do?"

CHAPTER 25

Alice

So we're all in danger now. Me, Julie, Jason — probably Dawn as well. How could Carl be so thoughtless — so reckless with our safety? It's not worth asking what he was thinking — he clearly wasn't thinking of us. But then it is Carl we're talking about.

It takes a few minutes for it all to sink in. The man at the door — he was checking us out. The bad guys think we were involved in the calamitous property deal, that somehow, we're helping Carl to get the money.

We could be next on their list.

I squeeze my eyes shut. "I can't believe this."

"I'm sorry, Alice," Jason repeats. "I'm as angry as you are. He was determined to drag me into all this somehow, and now he's made it impossible for me to stay out of it."

"Wait a minute — how long have you known this?"

"He came to the house, that night I couldn't sleep. He told me then."

"That was two days ago!"

"I wanted to tell you, but I didn't want to scare you, especially after that guy appeared at the door."

The panic rises in my chest. I know only too well what people like this are capable of. "You should have told me straight away, Jason. I'm not just scared — I'm terrified! They nearly killed Carl — do you think they won't do the same to you? And what about Julie, you need to warn her . . ." Now I'm panicking, the tears swelling in my eyes. "Jesus Christ, Jason! Those guys are evil. They won't think twice about threatening her. What if they break into her house? What if—"

I rock backwards and forwards, my arms crossed over my stomach. Jason comes round the table and crouches down in front of me. He unfolds my arms and holds me, stroking my hair.

"It's okay, Alice. Please don't. I won't let anything happen to you, or Mum, or Julie. I'm going to sort this out, I promise . . ."

I wipe the tears from my cheeks with the back of my hand. "But how, Jason? You're in danger too. What can you do?"

"I'll think of something."

"You're even beginning to sound like Carl. Something will turn up, isn't that what he always says?"

"Yes, and it usually does, doesn't it?"

"But it's never been like this! He's half-dead in hospital, and we're in danger now, too. We've got to tell the police — about the debt, the property deal — we have no option. We need to protect ourselves, and they might be able to scare them off, at least."

"Are you sure you want to do that, Alice?"

I hate the idea, of course I do. But we have to do something, and I don't want anyone else to get hurt. "I can't see what choice we have . . ."

"Okay. We'll call them tomorrow, as soon as I get home, all right?"

I nod. But I've got a horrible feeling we might be making things worse for ourselves.

CHAPTER 26

Jason

Rain spatters the pavements as Jason walks the half-mile home. It's the kind of gentle drizzle that penetrates everything, clinging to eyelashes, soaking into shoulders. A mist of tiny droplets shrouds the streetlamps, their light spilling in a haze onto the pavements. He blinks into the gloom, passing parked cars on his right, a terrace of run-down Victorian houses on his left. A car swishes through the puddles, its lights piercing the darkness ahead.

He's not looking forward to talking to the police. It'll be obvious he didn't tell them everything last time, and he risks getting into trouble for that. As he walks, he practises what he's going to say. It'll be lame, but he'll have to say he didn't think it was important, that Carl owes money to someone. At the moment, he can't think of anything better.

Turning into their street, he notices the same car idling a little way beyond their house. It's hard to see what it's like, the colour drained by the rain and the yellow of the streetlamps. The one outside the house hasn't worked for months and Jason's glad to see the porch lights defining the step to the front door, the front of the house lit up, both upstairs and downstairs. Alice must be home.

But something's wrong. Is it that he's on alert now because of Carl, or is it normal to see every window illuminated in the house? He and Alice are frugal with energy, conscious of the cost as well as the environment. It's not like Alice to be extravagant. Is she sending him a signal? He should check his phone, but as he hesitates on the pavement, the idling car roars into life like an angry bear preparing to pounce.

A back door opens. A man's leg emerges, a sturdy boot aiming for the ground. Jason turns and runs. Protected by the parked cars, he ducks down, his sneakers splashing through puddles, rainwater soaking his lower legs. About fifty metres back up the road is a hidden footpath, leading to the rear of the houses in this street — including theirs — providing access to garden gates and rubbish bins.

There's a shout behind him, the sound of feet running, muffled by the all-pervading wetness. Panting, he turns sharp right into the alleyway. It's pitch dark, ivy spilling over the fences on either side to form an incomplete, leafy roof, blocking out what little light might filter through from the road. He moves forward without a sound, hoping his pursuers are flummoxed by his sudden disappearance. The footpath is hard to spot even in daylight, and almost impossible to see if you don't know it's there. Even if they find it, they won't be able to spot him in the blanket of darkness beyond the street — unless they have a torch. He doesn't wait to find out.

At the fence at the bottom of his garden, he pauses for an instant to listen. There's not a sound other than the drip, drip of incessant rain from the trees around him. He climbs quickly, drops without a sound onto the ground next to the shed and starts to creep along the side fence towards the back of the house. All the lights are blazing on this side too. He's sure now, it's Alice's way of warning him.

A noise from behind. He freezes, turning slowly. The shed door is ajar. A hoarse whisper: "Jason, quick. Get in here, shut the door." Alice's face appears out of the gloom. He hurries in and closes the door. She's in his arms, cold and shaking.

"Thank God it's you," she whispers.

"Shh, it's okay, I'm here now. Keep still — they're right behind me."

They huddle in the space where Carl spent the night, on the same thin tarpaulin he tried to sleep under. Darkness surrounds them. Jason's ears ache with the intensity of listening. But there's only the dripping from the trees and the odd swish of a breeze in the bushes.

"They were here when I got back," Alice whispers after a few minutes. "Did you get my message?"

"No, I didn't check my phone. But I noticed you put all the lights on. Did you see their faces?"

"No. I was lucky, though — I already had my keys out. As soon as I saw the car, I was suspicious. Two men got out when they saw me turn into the house. They shouted at me to stop, but I managed to open the door and lock it behind me. Then I turned all the lights on. That must have deterred them, but I didn't wait to find out if they were going to break in, I ran to the shed."

Jason holds her tight. "Well done on the lights — I noticed straight away."

"What do we do now?"

"Call the police — and wait, I suppose. We can't go in until we're absolutely sure."

"I've alerted the whole street via WhatsApp," Alice says. "Someone's sure to tell them to move on."

"They'll leave once the neighbours start twitching their curtains. The power of Mrs Brown and Mrs Curtis knows no bounds."

Alice has stopped trembling now. "What if they come back?"

It's a good question — one Jason can't answer. "I doubt they will, now they know we're on to them. They'll be expecting us to call the cops."

The confidence in his voice belies his feelings.

There's no doubt about it now — they're in serious danger.

CHAPTER 27

Alice

We're back in the house at last. We waited, clutching each other in the dark for what seemed like an age, before Jason crept round the side of the house to check the street outside. Both the car and the men seem to have gone, so we've locked all the doors and windows and closed the curtains. I'm not reassured.

If I was frightened before, I'm terrified now. I know what people like this do when they want something.

"What if those guys are the ones that beat Carl up?"

Jason nods. He knows some of my past, but not all of it, and now's not the time. "I'm calling the cops," he says. "Unless you want to?"

I shake my head. "I'll only lose my temper. Talk to the DS on Carl's case — then let them put two and two together. Though they'll probably make three, knowing them."

"I'll tell them the rest, too, about the money."

"You must. Carl can't blame you for telling them now."

Jason searches on his phone. "DS Bennett — I'll call him now. Let's do it together."

"No — you do it. I don't want to make things worse."

Jason taps and puts his mobile to his ear. "DS Bennett, please," he says. "Jason Green. Yes, he'll know what it's about." After a moment, he moves into the sitting room. Snatches of conversation reach me in the kitchen.

"Yes, a dark-coloured four-door saloon, I'm not sure what make, it was hard to see in the dark. No, I was running — I didn't stop to get the registration number." A pause. "No. I didn't see their faces. It looked like more than two, but I didn't get the chance . . . Yes, his mother had a visit, too, before he was beaten up. Julie Jackson, yes. Yes, that's right."

I can hear a male voice talking, though I can't hear what's said. Then Jason says, "I have thought of something."

My ears prick up. I step closer to the door. I hope they go easy on him. Jason has a habit of prowling around when he's on the phone, particularly when he's nervous, and I can hear the floorboards creaking as he moves.

"Carl did mention he'd borrowed some money. From the wrong person, he said. No, I don't know the name — he called him Nick, but that wasn't his real name." There's a pause. "A property deal gone wrong . . . No, I have no idea what the company was called, he was being pretty cautious." Another pause. "No, he didn't mention that name — only Nick. No last name, no."

There's another pause as he listens, then he must have moved away from the door because I miss the next couple of replies. But I do catch him saying: ". . . a lot of money." He drops his voice, as if reluctant to say the words out loud. "A hundred thousand pounds." Another long pause, and I can just make out a male voice at the other end of the line. "Honestly — Carl was always borrowing money. I didn't think it was . . . Yes, it is a lot of money, but it was a genuine mistake on my part . . . Yes, I'm sorry, I didn't purposely—" A pause. "Yes, I understand that, but I had no intention of—" Another pause. "All right, thank you."

Jason returns, pocketing his mobile. "Well, that's done then. They said we should upgrade our security, and Julie and Mum too."

"So, you're okay? They're not going to haul you in for lying to them?"

Jason snorts. "I didn't lie, exactly, I just didn't tell them everything. They weren't happy, but they aren't hauling me in. I suppose they're more interested in catching these guys than in me missing something out."

"Did they say what they were doing to find them? Nothing, I bet." My cynicism towards the police knows no bounds.

"No, just that they were following up. But I think, given the amount of money in the frame, they'll take it seriously. They asked if Carl had mentioned a particular name, so maybe they have a lead."

"Oh? What was the name?"

"Neville — last name, I think. But it means nothing to me."

The blood drains from my face. I'm lucky to be standing at the sink, because a dark curtain begins to fall across my eyes. I lean forward to steady myself, turning on the tap with fumbling fingers.

"Alice? Are you okay?"

Jason sounds as if he's talking from within a bucket. There's a rushing in my ears.

"I–I'm fine, just need a drink." I cup my hands, not trusting myself to go to a cupboard to get a glass. I drink deep and splash my face with cold water. After a moment or two, I steady myself.

"I'm okay," I say as Jason's worried face appears through a haze of droplets.

But I'm not okay. I'm not okay at all.

CHAPTER 28

Alice

Neville. Just the sound of it makes me want to throw up. All the triggers come back at once — the horrible, nasal voice, the threats, the shame. I've buried the name, hidden it in the back of my mind, interred it. Until just now, as far as I knew, the Nevilles were cancelled — they were out of my life for good. Yet here they are, popping up again, and I'm right back to my childhood.

My mum was strict, conservative and religious. My father not so much, though he went along with her on most things. Mum was quite happy at home, cooking and looking after me and my sister while Dad went out to work. He was a civil servant — a manager at the West London branch of the Department of Social Security. I never really understood what he actually did.

My mum's social life was "The Church". She always said it with capital letters, to make it sound more important. She attended Sunday services throughout my childhood, dragging the rest of the family along too. On the other days of the week, she was at coffee mornings, helping to clean and tidy The Church, organising the summer fete or helping at fundraising events. The Church was her life, and she lived by its rules. My dad didn't get involved — he preferred the pub with his mates, when he was allowed, or an evening at the social club.

We weren't a well-off family, but my older sister Sarah and I weren't aware of any deprivation. We didn't have a car, but that didn't matter in our part of London. Christmas was a religious event, with just a few presents exchanged on the morning before church. We knew no different.

I was eight years old, Sarah just ten, when everything changed.

The doorbell rang. We were sitting at the kitchen table finishing our supper. Mum looked at Dad, her eyes wide with surprise. "Who could that be?" she said. We never had visitors in the evening. Morning coffee-time, yes — or at tea-time when my mum's friends would arrive with cake and biscuits. But nobody visited after supper.

I remember my dad's face. He had a strange look in his eyes, and I noticed a flush creeping up his neck, which I found fascinating. "Dad?" I said. I suppose I wanted him to explain this odd phenomenon, but he averted his eyes, dropped his napkin on the table and said, "I'll go. Everyone stay here."

We heard male voices at the door, then footsteps in the hall. They — whoever they were — disappeared into the lounge. This was unusual. Visitors rarely went in there — friends of our parents came into the kitchen, and on the rare occasions when our school friends were allowed over, we went upstairs to our rooms.

My sister and I looked at each other. Something wasn't right. "Mum?" Sarah said. "Who's that?"

"I–I really don't know." But she turned away, clearing the table without looking at us. "I'll wash up, girls, you go and do your homework."

We were astonished. It was always our job to wash up. We took it in turns to wash or dry, and though we hated it, we would mess about and laugh while we did it to relieve the boredom while our parents withdrew to the lounge to watch TV. But we were obedient girls, so we said nothing more and retreated to our rooms. At least, we did for a short time.

We decided to creep back to the stairs to keep watch. This occasion was unusual enough to make us curious, and so we waited on the top step, hoping to catch sight of the person or persons who'd interrupted our family's evening routine.

It seemed a long time before the door opened, and out came a tall policeman in full uniform, followed by a stranger in a long raincoat. We shrank back when they reached the front door, but as they left, the policeman put his tall hat on — to our delight — and the other man donned a brown felt hat. Neither of them shook my father's hand.

When they'd gone, my father stood looking at the front door for what seemed like a very long time before walking slowly back to the kitchen. He closed the door behind him. We looked at each other. The kitchen door was always open. Something very serious must be happening.

Our parents wouldn't tell us why a policeman had come to our house. We tried to find out, of course, and when our parents became tight-lipped and said it was nothing to do with us, we were even more intrigued. But all they would say was that it was grown-up business, something our father was dealing with, we were not to concern ourselves.

The atmosphere in our house changed from that day on. Dad had a permanent frown and Mum's mouth seemed to set in a hard line. Often the kitchen door would close when Dad got home from work, and we could hear muffled conversation, their voices low and urgent. They began to argue — something we'd never known before, and we started to feel miserable, confused, excluded from a family crisis. We spent a lot of time in our rooms.

Then, one horrible day, Dad packed a small bag, put it by the front door and sat us down in the kitchen. Mum was there, her face unreadable, her arms crossed over her chest. Dad said he was going away for a while, and we were to be good to Mum, not ask her too many questions, but not to worry, he would be home as soon as he could. He would write to us, he said, and we could write back, as long as we gave the letters to Mum to address and post. I asked if he'd come back for my birthday, which was only a few weeks away. When he said, gently, that it wouldn't be possible, I began to cry and plead with him, clinging to his arm. Mum pulled me off and told us to give him a kiss goodbye and go upstairs. By then Sarah and I were both crying and, to my surprise, Mum was too, though she tried not to show it.

The days turned into weeks and Dad didn't come home. Mum was tight-lipped. She told us to be patient, that Dad had no choice — he wanted to be with us, but he couldn't. She never said how long he'd be away, though we begged her to tell us. We asked why he had to be away, what was he doing, why couldn't we talk to him on the phone? In the end she got angry and told us to stop nagging her, we'd promised Dad we'd be good, and we weren't keeping our promise.

Gradually, as the weeks went on, we stopped asking. But we knew it was something bad, because Mum stopped seeing her friends, avoided people she knew on the street, and rushed away when she dropped us at school. On Sundays we'd creep into The Church at the back and leave just before everyone else. I felt ashamed, though I didn't know why.

Then, one day, the bombshell fell.

CHAPTER 29

Alice

Our father had gone away and wouldn't be back for a while. That was all we knew until the day I encountered Pete Neville. He was older than me by a couple of years and I steered clear of him when I could. He had a little gang that was always bullying and jeering at the weaker kids. Then one day I bumped into him by accident in the school corridor.

He rounded on me immediately, his mates gathering behind him. I muttered some kind of apology and tried to get past him, but he stood in the way, challenging me. "It's the little girly with the loser dad! How's he getting on in the nick, then? Hey, lads, she doesn't look like a hard nut, does she? But her dad's a criminal — he's in the Scrubs right now!"

I stepped backwards, my shoulder hitting the wall. I was confused and horrified, the tears not far away. What did he mean? I had no idea what "the nick" was, or "the Scrubs" — I was eight years old. But I knew this was bad. He spotted my reaction and turned the knife. "You didn't know? Hah! Baby girl didn't know her daddy's been banged up. He's in prison, baby girl. Everyone knows — it's all over the news." The lads around him laughed and pointed. They started to chant. "Baby girl, baby girl, Daddy's in the nick, Daddy's in the nick . . ."

By now I was trembling, cowering against the wall, tears coursing down my cheeks. Suddenly, a voice boomed from the end of the corridor. "Neville! Come here at once — and the rest of you." It was Mr Jones, the PE teacher, one of the only teachers in the school who had any control over the boys. "What the heck do you think you're doing? Do you think that makes you look big and strong, picking on a small girl? Well, it doesn't, it makes you idiots. Cowards. Big bullies. You're coming with me to the head's office — right now, all of you."

I slid down the wall, sobbing. "Are you okay?" Mr Jones came over and crouched down, a concerned look in his eyes. "Don't worry about them, they won't bother you again, I promise. Go to the school office, they'll look after you."

I nodded tearfully and obeyed. They were kind, but I was inconsolable. Of course I didn't tell them why I was so upset. The things Pete Neville had said raced through my mind. Was our dad really in prison? Disbelief, horror, denial — all kinds of horrible feelings swept over me. First I felt sick, then numb with shock.

Mum was called to come and collect me. She went in to see the head first, while my sister was summoned to comfort me. I couldn't speak, so she sat quietly with her arm around me until Mum came to get us.

She was white as a sheet. "Come on, girls," she said, not unkindly.

On the short walk home, Sarah kept asking what had happened. But Mum wouldn't talk until we got home. She sat us down at the kitchen table.

"Girls, I have something to tell you. Your father—" She broke off, her voice cracking. She swallowed with some difficulty. "Your father," she said in a stronger voice, "is easily led." We looked at her, a queue of unasked questions on our tongues. She held up a hand.

"So it's true," I whispered.

"What's true? What's true, Mum?" Sarah cried, a look of panic on her face.

"Dad's in prison," Mum said, swallowing hard. "I'm sorry, girls, I didn't want you to find out like this."

Sarah wailed — a horrible, anguished sound, and I went back to sobbing hysterically. Mum came round the table and held us, soothing us with small shushing sounds. "It's all right," she kept saying. "It's all right."

When at last the tears stopped, she handed us some tissues and sat down again.

Sarah gulped and took a deep breath. "Tell us what happened, Mum. What did he do?"

"He got in with a bad crowd, very bad indeed. There are evil people in this world, you know, who take advantage, who are selfish, and cruel, and—" She stopped, looking from me to Sarah, our tear-streaked faces, our pleading eyes. "I'll get to the point. Your father's a good man, he is. But he has — had — a friend, oh, he's not a friend anymore, you can't call him that, he's despicable, that Jack Neville — that boy's dad." Then, almost to herself, she added: "As they all are, the Nevilles. Criminals, gangsters, thugs — the lot of them. I told him, time and again, not to have anything to do with them. But would he listen?" She shook her head, her eyes glazed.

Then she seemed to come back to the moment. "He persuaded your father to put our life savings — all the money we had — into some kind of . . . scheme. I don't really understand how it was supposed to work. But he promised it would grow into much more money without your dad having to do anything. Your father got his other friends, and lots of people at work, to put their money into this scheme. But it turns out—" She took a deep breath. "It turns out the whole thing was illegal, and the police came after your dad. He was sent to prison for fraud. Just him — not the real criminal, Jack Neville. The police were useless — or corrupt, more like. Dad said Neville bribed them, or they were already under his thumb. Anyway, he got away scot-free."

I remember looking at Sarah then. Her face was as blank as mine must have been, her cheeks whiter than I'd ever seen them. I had no idea what "fraud" was, and it seemed that neither did she. But it must have been bad because our dad was in prison because of it.

On that day, I learned some new things. For instance, I learned that your friends can lead you into terrible trouble.

I also learned that you can't trust the police.

CHAPTER 30

Jason

His mobile flashes. He picks it up, flinching. Five missed calls, two voice messages, one text, all from Carl. He's being discharged today.

The first voicemail confirms his fears. Carl's voice is gravelly; he sounds as if he's still in pain. "I'm out of hospital today. They'll be after me, I know they will. I've got to do something. Call me."

The second, not long after: "If you won't help me, I'm going to get the money on my own. There's no other way out. Please call me."

The single text yells at him. *CALL ME!!!*

Jason runs his hands through his hair, holding clumps of it in his fingers. The last thing he wants to do is get embroiled in Carl's problems — especially while he's at work. He texts back: *Will call later — after work.*

After a couple of hours, he heads for home. His workplace is in the centre of Soho, the front door opening onto the pavement opposite a popular pub, where on warm nights the clientele spills out into the street. Today, though, the weather has deterred the usual knots of people on the pavement. Zipping up his jacket against the chilly wind, he turns towards the underground station, looking forward to a warm house and supper.

"Jason."

He stops mid-stride. He'd know that voice anywhere. Why hadn't he used the back entrance? He should have known Carl wouldn't leave him alone.

The figure before him limps slightly, its head down. A scarf hides half his face. The rest is almost hidden by a dark hood. Tinted glasses cover his eyes, a curl of yellow hair escapes onto his forehead.

"Carl?"

"Yeah, it's me. Keep walking."

Jason obeys, risking a sideways glance. "You're in disguise."

"I had to," Carl says, looking over his shoulder. "They were outside the hospital, waiting for me. A nurse smuggled me out. She did my hair, got me the clothes and the specs and pushed me out in a wheelchair. A new look, eh?" For a moment there's a flash of the old ebullient Carl. Then his head goes down again. "You have to help me now, Jason. They nearly killed me."

"I know. But honestly, there's nothing I can do. Go to the police or find your own way out of this."

Carl grabs Jason's arm, digging his fingers in so hard he can feel his skin bruising through his sleeve. His face is contorted with fear. "I'm not going to the cops. They'll bang me up and I'll be killed in the nick."

"Let go of my arm."

"No, you must listen to me." Carl looks around, his grip tightening. "Let's go in here." They stop at a pub on the corner. This one is not as popular — there are only a few punters inside, no queue at the bar. Carl pulls him inside.

"What can I get you?" The barman looks at Jason expectantly. Every instinct tells him to leave, not to be dragged into this again. But he gets his wallet out. There's no point expecting Carl to pay. "Coke, please," he says.

"Double Scotch on the rocks please, mate."

Jason almost laughs. Carl's attempt to disguise his voice is terrible — he sounds like a South American gangster. "If you think that's helping, think again," he says. "Keep talking like that and you'll have every criminal in town checking you out."

As soon as the drinks arrive, Carl grabs the whisky glass, taking a huge gulp. He snorts, almost choking as the liquid burns his throat.

"Steady on," Jason says. "I'm only staying for one, and I'm not intending to buy you another of those."

"Okay, okay. But I needed that."

"Before this goes any further, Carl . . . I'm serious about this. I'm not getting involved. I'll help you leave the country — I'll even pay for your ticket — but otherwise there's nothing I can do for you."

Carl's eyes blaze behind his glasses. "Yes, there is, Jason," he hisses. "You're forgetting something."

Despite himself, Jason hesitates. On the one hand, he's determined not to get involved; on the other, it looks like there's no way out. To keep his family safe, he has to help Carl. He feels like he's in a vice that's slowly being squeezed. He's being pushed, against every principle he's ever held, into helping someone commit a crime.

Perhaps he could lend Carl his car, just for a few days? As long as Carl uses false plates, Jason will be in the clear, and he can easily claim not to know why Carl needs it. But that won't work. Carl can't exactly park the car outside and unload the heavy gear — or carry it even a short distance. He'll need to be driven there and dropped off. It looks like Jason has no option.

The vice tightens.

For a moment, he stares into Carl's hopeful eyes. With a last effort, he says: "Are you trying to ruin my life, Carl?"

Carl snorts. "No, I'm trying to save mine."

Jason knows what he's thinking. *Like I saved yours.* It's hopeless. He feels his shoulders drop in defeat. "Look, I've got to go," he says. "Tell me where the house is."

"So, you'll help?"

"I'm not saying that. Send me the address. I'll think about it."

Outside the cafe, the fresh air hits him like a punch in the belly. He barely makes it into the alley round the corner, where he retches until his throat aches.

CHAPTER 31

Alice

I wake with a start. Jason's side of the bed is empty, but it's still dark outside. I reach for my mobile. Five thirty. I groan. There's no sound from the bathroom, no light from the landing, but the bedroom door is ajar. We always close it at night.

I'm worried about him. When he came back from work yesterday he was quiet, distracted. He seemed unable to focus on anything I said, and I know it's all about Carl. He was waiting for him after work, and they had a drink together. I'm pretty sure Carl's putting pressure on him. God, I wish he'd just get out of our lives.

Cursing, I swing my legs to the floor, my feet feeling for my slippers. I'm so tired. Why does he have to wake me up with his worrying? Muttering under my breath, I wrap a robe around me and pad downstairs.

In the sitting room, Jason's asleep on the sofa in a tangle of throws and cushions. My mood softens at his sleeping face. A slight frown hovers around his forehead but his mouth is slack, one cheek ballooning out over a cushion, giving him a childish look. It's hard to be angry with him. He's a good person, even if he's too soft to resist his scoundrel of a friend.

I straighten the blankets, taking care not to wake him, and trudge back upstairs. On the landing, I pause to look at the full moon, casting its eerie light over the garden, making silvery tracks over the roof of the house behind. My eyes take a little time to adjust, but as I turn to go, a movement in the bushes down below startles me. A cat, perhaps? The next-door neighbours have two, and they're always on the prowl through the gardens in the street. But then I freeze, my scalp contracting with a frisson of fear. It's too big for a cat — it's a man. If it wasn't for the moonlight, I would never have seen him — he's all in black and he's creeping towards the house.

In an instant, my feet are taking me down the stairs, so fast they barely touch the carpet. "Jason!" I call as loudly as I dare. I run to him, shaking him by the shoulder, my eyes on the back window. "Jason, quick! There's someone in the garden — wake up—"

Jason's awake in a flash, his eyes widening with shock. We creep together towards the window. In that fraction of a second, I find myself worrying that I'm in bare feet and a robe and I might not be able to run too fast, then wonder what on earth I'm thinking.

At first, we can see nothing from the window. But a moment later, there's a sudden movement in the shadows — an almighty crash from the kitchen, the sound of breaking glass, a massive thump.

I clutch at Jason's arm in terror. "Christ, Jason, what was that?" He holds me behind him, still peering through the window, as a black shadow races across the grass to the darkness at the far end of the garden. We freeze. I'm listening so hard my ears hurt. But there's no sound from the kitchen. Jason steps across to the fireplace, grabbing a poker. "Stay behind me," he whispers. Crouching, we move together towards the kitchen door. All is quiet.

"Careful, there's broken glass," Jason says. He steps through and I follow, treading carefully, keeping to the edges of the room. When he turns the light on, I'm dazzled for a moment, as if someone has pointed a flashlight into my eyes. The scene before me unfolds, bit by bit. A huge lump of concrete sits in the middle of the floor. The sheer heft of it is incredible: it must have taken enormous strength just to lift it, let alone to throw it through our window. Shards of glass are scattered everywhere around it, in the sink, on the worktops, even as far as the table.

But that's not the worst of it. Next to it, a grubby piece of rope around its neck, is a dead cat.

My hands fly to my face in horror. I know this cat — it belongs to Mrs Curtis from over the road. It's a regular visitor to our garden. I run to the front door and grab my boots, wrestling with them and cursing in my haste. I grab Jason's Wellington boots and race back to the kitchen. "Here, put these on."

Shaking, I loosen the rope from the cat's neck and cradle it in my arms. Its head flops over my arm. Its neck is broken. Tears rush to my eyes. "Mrs Curtis will be devastated. Poor thing."

"Wrap it up and put it outside — here, I'll do it. We shouldn't touch anything else. Go and put some clothes on. I'm going to take some pictures."

"For the police?"

"We must, Alice. This is out of control now."

I take a deep breath. He's right, though my heart sinks. This is clear evidence that we're in the frame.

I dress hurriedly and run back downstairs. Jason is outside, assessing the damage. "Come and look," he says.

Outside the back door he's staring at the back wall of the house, a torch in his hand. Beside the destroyed window, someone has scrawled a muddy message in big letters. *YOU'RE NEXT.*

CHAPTER 32

Alice

By the time the police arrive, I'm panicking about making the kitchen secure for the night. I wonder if there's an emergency service for people who've had their windows broken in the small hours.

Two tired-looking uniforms go through to the kitchen while I wait in the sitting room. Jason talks them through what happened, shows them our destroyed kitchen window and the chunk of concrete on the broken tiles. They examine the scrawl on the outside wall — and he has to unwrap the poor cat so they can inspect it. For God's sake. Surely the cat can't offer any clues? I'd laugh if I wasn't so upset.

I compose myself when they come to question me. I keep to the facts, and manage not to antagonise them, though it's a stretch when they ask if I think this is anything to do with Carl being beaten to within an inch of his life. But I take a deep breath and keep my face neutral. "Yes, I do." Surprise, surprise.

But they're not too stupid, after all. "Why do you think they're threatening you?" one of them says. She's a young officer, probably not more than twenty-five, but she listens, at least. I hesitate because I don't know exactly what Jason's told them. I glance at Jason, who's leaning against the doorjamb, listening. The policewoman looks up. "In your own words, please."

"I understand," I say carefully, "that Carl may have . . . given the impression that Jason was going to help get the money. Or that Jason has the money, I'm not sure."

"Why do you think that might be?"

I shrug. "I don't know, maybe because we have a house and decent jobs — and Carl's never owned a property, or earned a salary in his life? Who knows what he's thinking?" Jason makes a tiny gesture, his hand facing the floor. *Be careful.* I drop my shoulders and breathe. "But we have no money, it all goes on the mortgage and the bills." I just want them out of my house. Years of hating them, mistrusting them, fearing them, even, are hard to put behind me. I find myself grinding my teeth.

The officer nods at me. She consults her device, on which she's been taking notes.

"What are you doing to find these guys?" I say, trying not to sound aggressive. "They're obviously dangerous. What happened tonight — it's terrifying. We don't want to end up beaten to a pulp, like our friend."

"Of course not. We are making enquiries . . ."

Enquiries. As if that will placate me. "Are they leading anywhere?" I try to keep the sarcasm from my voice.

"All I can say is, we have a number of leads and we're following up as fast as we can."

"In the meantime, we have to hope they don't get to us like they got to Carl?" That prompts another gesture from Jason, still standing in the doorway.

"As I've said to Mr Green here, my advice to you is, get a dog. With a big bark, preferably. If you can't, or you don't want to do that, get a monitored alarm as soon as you can," the other officer says. "It won't stop chunks of concrete, but it will make a villain think twice. It'll give you some protection — and peace of mind. Some companies will give you priority, as you've been broken into already. Try this one." He hands me a business card. "We'll put a marker on your address with details of this incident. If you're worried, call 999 — the police handler will know what's happened this evening. Keep your eyes and ears open, and when you go out, go together if you can."

"Thanks," Jason says. "We'll get an alarm installed straight away."

The female officer turns to me again. "One last question for you, Ms Mayfield, if that's okay — does the name Neville mean anything to you?"

I'm expecting it, fortunately. I keep my voice steady and my gaze on her eyes, pausing for a moment as if considering. "Absolutely nothing." She holds my gaze for a few moments, then nods and types into her notepad. My shoulders ache with tension.

It seems like hours before they leave. Before they do, one of them helps Jason shore up the window temporarily with a piece of wood left over from the kitchen refurb. It's solid enough, and it'll do until morning, but I don't imagine I'll get a moment's sleep until it's replaced. With reinforced glass, preferably.

"And please, keep us informed of anything unusual. It could be important," the other one says.

I close the door firmly behind them.

CHAPTER 33

Jason

After a night without rest, Jason starts the day early with the gruesome task of returning the dead cat to its owner. He wraps the limp body in a soft towel and crosses the road, dreading the next few minutes.

As he feared, Mrs Curtis breaks down, tears welling as Jason stammers out the story of last night. He blames kids "from outside the area" and tells her the police are on to them, to reassure her she's in no danger. He offers to dig a grave for the cat in her garden later this evening. It's the least he can do.

Cradling the bundle in her arms, Mrs Curtis nods, her lower lip trembling. "That would be very kind," she whispers. "Thank you."

Jason walks to his car in a grim mood. The attack on the house has completed the circle in his mind. His family is in grave danger, and he needs to do something about it, fast. There's no way the police will act quickly enough to keep them safe.

The only way out is to help Carl steal the money. He punches the postcode into the sat nav in his car.

From the look of the street alone, it's clear that Needham's wealthy. It's one of those private streets in a suburb of London where the trees are tall and the traffic sparse. Speed bumps every few metres to slow the cars. Big gates, high walls and entry systems.

He walks with intent, though not fast. The last thing he wants to do is attract attention — his aim is simply to get a feel for the area and, if possible, a glimpse of the house. He walks up one side of the street and down the other, pausing to look at his phone as if he's following directions. The house, a square mock-Georgian building, has two storeys and a flat-roofed porch with white columns. To the front of the house, a short drive is flanked by curves of grass, dotted with shrubs and bushes. That's all he can see in a momentary glance as he walks past.

Every so often a car passes by. He wonders if Needham goes out every day. Does he still work? With all that money, he surely doesn't need to. Jason knows so little about this man — if he were a "proper" burglar, he'd do a lot more homework. But he's not and has no intention of becoming one. Even coming here was a bad idea.

He considers hanging around to see if there's any move-ment at the house but decides it's too dangerous — he can't risk being seen. There's not much else he can do to familiarise himself, so he walks the length of the street again, turning at the end to see where he might linger to drop Carl off. Tonight, he'll drive here, to gauge the timings and identify a safe spot to wait.

He still can't believe he's going to do this. He's under no illusions — if Carl's caught, Jason will be an accessory. Simple as that. His strong sense of loyalty to a friend would mean nothing to the police. Even the excuse that he was protecting his family wouldn't hold water. He might get a suspended sentence if they believe he's simply the driver. But maybe not. Surely a driver is an accessory if a crime's com-mitted and he helps the perpetrator escape?

If Jason gets a criminal record, that's his career over, his life chances severely limited. He would almost certainly lose Alice too. He hardly dares think about her.

But he's got to do it, whether he likes it or not, and now he wants to get it over with as soon as possible. Luckily, Carl does too — the sooner the better for him. It might even be in the next day or two — the weather forecast promises clear skies at night for at least two or three days. The moonlight might be of some help.

A massive burden has settled on Jason's shoulders since all this started, and now it's even worse. If he tells Alice he's going to help Carl in this . . . madness, she'll be furious with him, whatever danger they might be in. She may even move out, temporarily or — he can hardly bear to think about it — permanently.

CHAPTER 34

Alice

Something's going on with Jason, I know it.

"You've hardly spoken all evening," I say at last. "And you've barely eaten. Something's going on, I know it is. Isn't it? Tell me, Jason, please."

I can almost see his mind running through possible explanations. He takes a deep breath and lets it out slowly. "I'm going to help Carl get the money." His voice is flat, emotionless. As if it's final. No consultation. He's made this decision without me, and there's nothing I can do about it. He's going to do something bad — so bad he could end up in prison.

I feel the blood drain from my cheeks. My father's face flashes before my eyes and I'm eight years old again. Disbelief, fear, and a sense of betrayal battle it out in my heart.

Jason carries on, his eyes swerving away from mine. "I know you don't want me to. I'm sorry."

I close my eyes, my body clenching. The long silence that follows is broken only by the sound of the cooker ticking as it cools. Nausea rises, dizziness grips me, my stomach churns. A voice in my head says, "No, no, not again," over and over.

I stand abruptly, the chair behind me scraping across the floor with an ear-splitting screech. Jason flinches.

"I knew it — I knew it. How could you? You promised, Jason!"

He slumps in his chair, unable to meet my eyes. I'm not sure he did promise, but that's irrelevant. He knew very well I didn't want him to get involved, but he went ahead without listening to me. That's an insult, and it hurts. My stomach twists, my throat aches with the effort not to cry.

For a moment, I want to get out of there — leave the room, the house, hide from this horrible thing that's threatening to tear us apart. But I can't.

I resist the urge, sit down with a thump. I swallow, hard. "Right. Tell me the truth, Jason. What have you agreed to do?"

"Do you really want to know?"

"Believe me, I do."

He starts to tell me. The words pour out of him in a monotone, as if he can hardly bear to hear them himself. He stares at the floor. As I listen, it's as if the temperature in the room drops. He tells me about a builder friend of Carl's who's amassed a pile of money, a drunken conversation with a mate. The words *cash*, *steal*, *break-in*, *code* echo around my head. I barely hear the rest. The air feels cold and damp, and I shiver. My body stills. I'm stunned into silence.

Jason still won't look at me. "All I'm doing is driving him there and back. I'm not going into the house, I'm not taking anything from anyone, I don't want to know what he does with the money."

"That doesn't make it okay." My voice shakes with emotion.

He hangs his head. "I know."

"Where is it? The house?"

"He sent me the address. It's near Wimbledon."

I give him a piercing look.

"Well, if I'm driving there, I need to know."

"When?"

"The next couple of days. Maybe even tonight."

"Oh God." My hand flies to my mouth. I can't believe it. So soon.

It's sheer madness; I have to make him see it. I pace around the room, my voice hard and emotionless, firing questions at him, trying to make him see all the things that could go wrong. I don't expect him to answer, and he doesn't even try.

"For God's sake, Jason, don't do this! What the hell are you thinking? You know as well as I do, it won't work — not in a million years."

"I know it's a risk, but there's a chance he'll get away with it — there is."

I sigh, a deep, shuddering breath from the depths of my body. "A risk? You're completely mad, Jason. You know he'll reel you in even further, and you're already in too far. If he's caught, you can bet your life he won't protect you. I can't believe you. Why can't you tell him to fuck off?"

"He has nobody else."

I let out a groan — more like a scream — of frustration. "That's no reason to ruin your life! And mine too, by the sound of it — and your mum's, not to mention poor Julie. Honestly, Jason, this is unbelievable. You agreed to do this, without talking to me first, without thinking of us, our life together, our future. What if you end up in prison, like my dad? What do you think that will do to me?"

"I'm sorry, Alice." He hangs his head.

There's a long pause. "You're sorry, but you're still going to do it."

"Sorry," he whispers, his voice cracking. There seems to be nothing else he can say.

"Stupid question, of course. Anything for Carl."

He looks at me then. "It's not just for Carl. It's for you, and Mum, and Julie. We're all in danger. If he gets the money, it'll be over. That's why I'm doing it."

"Well, I can't condone it. It doesn't matter that we're in danger. We can deal with that, we can move, we can — I don't know. But I don't want you to ruin all our lives."

"I won't, I promise."

"But how can you promise? You can't, can you? I want nothing to do with it. If I had somewhere to go, I'd leave." I stand in front of him, every muscle tensed, my hands in fists by my sides.

Jason flinches. "Don't leave, Alice, please."

"Right now, I wish I could, believe me. I'm going upstairs. Please don't follow me."

I stride towards the door.

Jason's voice follows me. "Don't tell anyone what Carl's doing, will you?"

I hesitate, my mouth twisting. "What? Is he all you care about?"

"No, of course not. I care about you, much more. But it's important — I'm begging you, Alice. Don't tell anyone — not even Mum. Please — you have to keep this to yourself."

"Okay, okay. I won't tell." Now I just want to get out of there, be by myself for a while. I can't look at his face anymore.

"You must promise me . . ."

I let out a frustrated groan. "For God's sake, Jason — I promise! I won't tell a soul. Happy now?"

"Thanks." It's barely audible.

Tears flood my eyes as I leave the room.

CHAPTER 35

Alice

The night is long and terrible. Much later, I hear Jason moving around, the door to the spare room closing.

In the morning, I'm wrecked. Groaning, I turn my face to the pillow. What am I going to do? I have to stop this happening — I can't sit by and watch it all go wrong. I have to talk to someone — but I can't talk to my best friend, because that's Jason. I do have other friends, of course, but nobody I want to entrust this to — I'd feel too disloyal to Jason.

There's only one person I can confide in. Even though he's sworn me to secrecy over this, she deserves to know. Between us we might even be able to stop him. It'll be worth the betrayal.

This morning I'll talk to Dawn. I hope she'll know what to do.

I leave early, checking the street both ways as I walk the short distance to Dawn's house. The street is busy with commuters hurrying to and from the station, and there's a constant churn of buses and taxis from the main road nearby. As far as I can tell, there's nobody interested in me.

I can see by the curtains in the upstairs window that she's up and about, so I take the path down the side of the house and knock on the back door. I can hear sounds inside, a man's voice reading the news on the radio, cupboards closing.

"Door's open," Dawn calls.

I step inside. Dawn's at the kitchen sink, her back to the door. She glances over her shoulder and smiles. She's still in her dressing gown and slippers, her hair rumpled. "Come in, sit down," she says. "I've made some tea. Would you like breakfast?"

She turns, and for a moment I'm shocked. She seems to have shrunk since I last saw her. Purple smudges underline her eyes; the skin on her face is slack and grey. The hands that hold the mugs of tea shake slightly. She sets them on the table.

"Are you okay, Dawn? I'm sorry to come so early—"

"I'm fine." She smiles. "You're not used to seeing me looking such a mess. I couldn't get to sleep last night — I was awake for hours. Menopause, probably. Women have to put up with so much — a curse in childbearing years, then another one when the first one stops. It's not a fair world, is it?"

"You're right about that."

"Toast?"

"Not for me, thanks. No breakfast. I came to — well, the reason I'm here is . . ." I stutter, helpless. I had the words all ready, but now, with Dawn looking so fragile, it's hard to find them.

"It's Jason, isn't it? You can tell me."

"It is Jason, and it might be upsetting, I'm afraid. I'm not supposed to tell you. He swore me to secrecy, but I'm going to break my promise, because if I don't, he's going to do something really stupid. You have to help me stop him, Dawn."

This time, I don't spare the details. If I'm going to betray Jason to his mum, I might as well tell her everything.

111

Carl's plan, the bent builder and how they met. How they were drinking mates, until they fell out. The secret stash, the scribbled drawing of the house with the room marked *MONEY* — the safe, even the code. That Jason has agreed to help Carl steal the money.

As the story spills out, Dawn becomes stiller and stiller, and all the colour in her face drains away. But for the slight rise and fall of her chest, her body is frozen.

There's a long silence before she exhales, a long whistle of disbelief.

"Blimey," she says at last. If the situation wasn't so appalling, I might have laughed.

"Blimey indeed. What can we do, Dawn?"

"I have absolutely no idea. It's hard to take it all in. Poor old Carl. What a mess he's got himself into."

"Poor Carl? Damn him, more like! I'm sorry for Jason. He can't say no to Carl, can he — and that rat knows it."

"It's always been like that. I know which one I'd rather have for a son. He needed a father in his life, to sort him out."

"Some men have a lot to answer for. I mean, men like his dad — shirking responsibility for their kids. But he never got into real trouble before, did he? Not that I know, anyway. This is on a completely new level."

"It does seem to be."

"I'm sorry to say this, but I'm so disappointed in Jason, Dawn. He has always stood up for his principles, and that's one of the things I admire about him. Normally he's unshakeable. But when Carl comes back into his life, it all falls apart." I take a deep, shuddering breath. "What if he ends up in prison?"

Dawn places a thin hand over mine. "Come on, Alice. It may still be okay. Let's try and work something out. I'll talk to Jason—"

"You can't — he swore me to secrecy. He even told me not to tell you, specifically. I had to promise. If he knows I told you, he'll be furious."

Dawn waves a hand. "Okay, okay, I won't talk to him. Not yet, anyway. Let's talk to Carl, instead."

I'm startled. "Talk to Carl? Even if we can track him down, do you think we'd have a chance of stopping him? If he doesn't get the money very soon, I dread to think what will happen. We've been agonising over it, me and Jason, and we can't see any way out of it."

"You're right, he has to get some money, at least to buy him time." She stops for a moment to think. "Do you know how to contact him?"

"I think Jason has a number for him, but I doubt he'd give it to me. Carl's still in the area, though, I'm pretty sure, because the house he wants to rob — I can't believe I'm saying this — isn't far. But I don't know where he's living. Probably in someone's shed, without their knowledge."

"Do you know where the house is, the one they're planning to burgle?"

"Near Wimbledon, Jason said."

"I suppose Julie might have Carl's number. Let's see what we can find out."

"She doesn't need to be drawn into this mess, too. I'm already feeling bad enough, telling you."

"Don't worry, I'll text. Innocently." Dawn's mobile is already in her hands.

When she's finished, she puts two slices of bread in the toaster and sits down again. "Right," she says. "So, when we do find him — and we will — we can do a number of things."

"Really?" Dawn has a way of surprising me.

"We can try again to persuade him not to do the burglary."

I shake my head. "We've been through all this a thousand times. He's dead set on it. I'm beginning to feel it's all hopeless, and there's nothing we can do."

Dawn raises a hand to show she understands. "Okay. He's not going to change his mind now, so we can cross that one out. Next idea: we lock him in a room and refuse to let him out."

I snort. "We'd have to let him out one day."

"Sadly, we would — and it's kidnapping, and that would make us criminals. And we might be putting ourselves

113

in danger from the bad guys. We can't do it." She hesitates for a moment. "We could tell the police — knock the whole idea on the head."

"What?" I say, aghast. "Put the police onto Jason? He'd never forgive me! I don't — I can't do that, Dawn." I feel the blood rush to my face. I love Jason, I can't do that to him. He'd never survive prison, he—

"I know. It would stop them doing the burglary, but it wouldn't help the situation, in a lot of ways. Last resort then?"

"Absolutely last resort." Relief washes over me.

"Okay," Dawn says, patting my arm. "Don't worry — I'm looking at all our options. What about these guys he owes money to? Can we talk to them?"

I gape at her. "They're thugs, Dawn. They almost killed Carl, and I'm sure they wouldn't hesitate if they get another chance. They've already threatened us, too. There's no way they're interested in talking. The simple act of looking for them would be dangerous. Don't even think about it."

"Threatened you? What did they do?" I tell her about the broken window, leaving out the gruesome detail of the dead cat and the chilling message. Even my toned-down story makes her gasp.

"Oh my goodness. You must have been so frightened. I hope you called the police?"

"Of course. They came to the house, took details. Not sure what else they could do. But we're getting an alarm as soon as possible."

"We have to do something, Alice — this is terrible. I can give him some money to get out of the country. Probably enough to get a long way. How about that? Surely that gives him the best chance?"

"It's generous of you — thank you — but no need. It seems it won't help. Carl's convinced these guys will still catch him, even in another country — they're part of a world-wide criminal gang, he says. I don't think he's being melodramatic, either."

"And it wouldn't stop them threatening you, either." She shakes her head. "But we must stop this burglary. Could we talk to the guy — the one Carl wants to rob?"

"Talk to Needham? That's a thought. I suppose Jason must know where he lives. But he's not going to tell me, is he? And anyway, what will we do — knock on his door and say, you don't know us, but we know someone who is going to try and rob you? As far as I know, Needham's pretty dodgy too. We've got no idea how he'd react — and how would it help?"

"I suppose he'd move his money. Then Carl can't steal it. But you're right, it doesn't achieve anything much. Carl would find the money gone, but he could still get caught breaking into the house and Jason would still be an accessory. And Carl would still owe the money to the really bad guys."

"I'm out of ideas, Dawn. I've already been over this again and again in my head."

"I'm sure you have. Look, let's find Carl first and try to talk some sense into him. Perhaps he'll ignore us and go ahead anyway. But we can ask him not to involve Jason, surely that's worth a try."

"Okay. That's something, at least."

"And let's try to find out where the house is. The more we know about it, the better."

"How can I do that without Jason being suspicious?"

Dawn shrugs. "I don't know. But I do know you're resourceful — you'll think of something."

CHAPTER 36

Jason

Only a couple of days to go before Carl's ready to press the button. Jason's still resisting his attempts to run through the details. It'll be a gamble, a game of chance, and Carl will be crossing his fingers that he can use the climbing equipment, that the plan of the house is right, that Needham sticks to his routine, that the alarm is easy to disable. That the money is indeed where it's supposed to be. The chances of the whole thing going wrong are seriously high. Or to look at it the other way, the chances of it succeeding are close to zero.

But on the other hand, there is a chance.

Jason's already stretched nerves are at breaking point, and Alice isn't speaking to him. There's a mountain of things he'd like to say to her, but he can't. Seeing her is agony. She's avoiding him, eating separately, spending the evenings upstairs without him. All he wants to do is fold her in his arms and tell her everything will be all right. But he can't, and it might not be.

The front door bangs. He steps into the hall as she removes her coat. She doesn't say hello or look at him, and there's an awkward moment when she attempts to pass him to get to the stairs.

"Sorry." He moves to one side.

"It's okay," she says, avoiding his gaze. She takes the stairs two at a time, as if rushing to get away. Sadness settles onto his shoulders.

"Can I get you a drink?" he says to her retreating back.

"Er, yes. Tea, please."

He heads for the kitchen, his feet dragging. How can such a close relationship become so brittle, so quickly? He longs for her to sink into the sofa beside him in the sitting room, to take his hand. For them to sit in comfortable silence, watching a movie or reading. For that morning moment when he wakes up, her ruffled head beside him, her body warming his . . . but he stops himself. It's only making things worse.

His mobile pings and lights up on the work surface. He ignores it, all his focus on Alice moving around above his head.

"Jason," she calls from the top of the stairs. "Can you help? There's some stuff on the top of the wardrobe I can't reach."

In their bedroom, which has become hers in the last couple of days, she points to a box on the top of the wardrobe. "Could you get that one down, please — and the one behind it, too. I'll go and make the tea."

Wondering what she's looking for in boxes that haven't been opened for months, Jason pulls up a chair and grabs the first one. The dust-coated cardboard is flimsy, the contents heavy, and he struggles to lift it over the raised edge along the front of the wardrobe. Books, perhaps? Why does she need this? But he's not going to ask. If she wants the box, he'll get it for her, no questions asked. The one behind is even more awkward and takes a few minutes to manoeuvre to the edge and lift down. He leaves both boxes on the bed without opening them and goes down to the kitchen.

Alice is looking through a small pile of post he brought in this evening but couldn't face checking. The tea is made and she's already halfway through her mugful.

"The boxes are on the bed," he says, willing her to look at him.

"Right," she says, without lifting her eyes. "Thanks."

117

On the way back up the stairs, she turns. "Jason, wait. You need to see your mum — I'm worried about her. She's not looking well."

Jason nods. "I will, I'll go tomorrow."

She disappears back up the stairs.

A wave of sadness drifts over him again. She won't even stay in the room with him to finish her drink.

He's ruined everything, and he doesn't have a clue what to do about it.

CHAPTER 37

Jason

On the way to his mum's, his phone buzzes. Carl.

"We're on for tomorrow night, then." Carl's hoarse whisper resonates in his ear, traffic noise in the background blurring the words.

Jason swallows with difficulty, his mouth dry. He can't believe it's going to happen. In the back of his mind, there's still a grain of hope that it won't — that something will miraculously arrive to solve Carl's problem. But Jason doesn't believe in miracles, and he must get this over and done with. He imagines tomorrow, when Carl will have successfully stolen the money, and nobody has caught them and Carl is paying off his debt. Alice will forgive him; everyone will be safe, and life will return to normal. He daren't imagine anything else.

"You've got the equipment?" Jason asks.

"Yeah, no problem. It's bloody heavy, all that rigging stuff. No way I could carry that for too long, not with my ribs."

Yet another reason this could go horribly wrong. "Are you sure you want to go ahead with this?" It's pointless, but he can't resist saying it.

"I'll take some painkillers before I go."

"How much stuff is there?"

"Tons. They leave a bag ready for the next job. That's what I took."

"You didn't check what was in it?"

"No need. I know what they put in there."

"Do you need to bring it all?"

"Dunno yet. Might do."

Irritation stabs at him, but he tries not to show it. "Check it, Carl. You won't need all of it. Keep it as light as possible."

"Yeah, yeah. It'll be fine."

Jason swallows an angry retort. Carl's doing his usual thing, even now, with his life at stake. He's not taking anything seriously, hoping it will all work out somehow. He can only pray that Carl's knack of getting away with things kicks in. The whole scheme is steeped in risk and the rock in his stomach is getting heavier by the moment.

"Look, I know you think you're prepared, but how about finding a wall somewhere, having a practice?" Before he's even finished saying it, he knows it's a stupid idea.

Carl snorts. "Right. In the park, do you think? Or at my mum's house? Where am I going to do that then, so nobody notices?"

"Okay, I get it. But sort the stuff out, chuck out the heavy things if you don't need them. You'll be quicker, and it'll be less painful."

"You said." There's a note of annoyance in his tone.

"Right." It's not worth pushing him any more. Carl will do the minimum — he's always been like that. He has never practised anything in his life.

"Tomorrow then," Jason says. "I'll be at the place we agreed, five minutes ahead of time. Don't be late. If anything goes wrong, message me, don't call — use WhatsApp."

"Yes. See you then."

"Right." He cuts the call with a terrible sinking feeling, like he's boarded a boat in the face of a tornado.

It's too late now. They're committed, and they're going ahead.

CHAPTER 38

Jason

He studies the people on the platform before stepping onto the train. It feels strange — over-dramatic, even — to behave like this, but he can't take any chances with his mum's safety. He decides to get off the train a stop early, to be absolutely sure. Dozens of other people alight at the same station, pouring up the steps and out into the drizzle. Some turn in the same direction as him. He stops at a shop window, pretending to look at his phone, watching the reflection. Only one figure stops too, a man in a baseball cap, his face obscured, also checking his phone. It could be nothing, but he's taking no chances.

He takes a circuitous route, checking his back at every turn. The slim figure stays some distance behind him, but it's always there, sauntering along, glancing to one side when he looks. Now he's certain he's being followed. Luckily, he knows the area well. He turns into a short street and takes off, sprinting to the junction at the end. There he turns — the man is still out of sight. He runs to the end of the next street, and the next, until he's out of breath and heaving. At last, he heads towards his mum's house. By the time he gets there he's soaked through.

It's no more than a week or so since he saw her, but when Dawn opens the door, he can see why Alice is worried. She looks old all of a sudden, her clothes a little too large. There's a slight wobble in her step as he follows her to the kitchen.

"I'll do the tea." He takes the kettle from her hands. "Sit down, you look tired."

The truth is, she looks terrible, but he daren't say it.

"I'm glad to see you, Jason."

"You too. How've you been?"

"Oh, you know. Perhaps a bit under the weather, nothing to worry about. Tell me what's going on with you. You're much more interesting than me."

He tells her a bit about work as he makes the tea, but she seems distracted, and his heart's not in it. He barely knows what he's saying.

"Tell me what's happening with Alice," she says at last. "I know she's angry with you. She's a lovely person, Jason, you mustn't lose her."

He feels his shoulders droop. "I know. I don't want to lose her. But, you know, she has a thing against Carl, and I've been trying to help him with this corner he's got himself into—"

His mum nods slowly. "With money?"

He glances at her, but there's no sign of any hidden message. "I've given him a bit. Not much, because I don't have much, and anyway there's no way he can repay me. I'm trying to get him back on track. He's got no work and nowhere to live except his mum's, and he can't live there until he sorts out this . . . problem."

"So where is he?"

"We don't know. Living rough somewhere probably."

"That's not good." Dawn shakes her head. "But poor Julie has put up with him for too long. It's time he learned not to lean on everyone else. Including you."

He sighs. "I know, Mum. But he is — he was — my friend."

122

There's a pause. "Not anymore?"

"No." He can't look her in the eye. "Not anymore. He's let me down once too often."

"I must say, I'm relieved to hear you say that. He's a bit of a parasite, that one, and it's not going to change now." She pulls herself up from her chair with difficulty, as if her legs can't quite hold her, and opens a cupboard. "Now let me see. Here it is! I've made your favourite. Lemon drizzle cake."

"Oh, Mum, you shouldn't put yourself out for me. But it looks — and smells — amazing, as always."

"Big piece then?" She places a generous slice in front of him.

"Aren't you having any?"

"I'm not getting enough exercise to make me hungry these days."

"Not given up on the classes, have you?"

She brushes a lock of hair from her eyes. "Not given up. Just haven't been for a while, I've been a bit tired."

His anxiety ratchets up a few notches. Ever since he was a small boy at nursery school, his mum's been as regular as clockwork with her fitness classes. At first, she saw them as a respite from being a mother but found herself enjoying them and has never stopped.

"Have you seen a doctor, Mum?" He tries to keep the note of anxiety from his voice.

"Yes, everything's fine. No need to worry about me. You concentrate on sorting things out with Alice. You'll never find another like her."

CHAPTER 39

Alice

"I've found Carl. At least, I've got his number."

"I knew you'd do it," Dawn says.

"It was easy. I distracted Jason into moving some boxes and checked his phone. There was only one number unidentified that he'd had a conversation with. He never takes unidentified calls. Carl's got a burner phone."

"What's that?"

"A disposable mobile. You can make and receive calls — and texts, I think — but nothing else. Criminal gangs use them. They get rid of them once they've used them and they can't be traced."

"Let's hope he hasn't chucked it already. We'd better call him right away. See if he'll meet."

"Yes, but if he won't meet, we'll have to do it on the phone. They may even be planning to do it tonight."

There's a whispered curse from Dawn's end of the line. "You're right. Alice — can you come here now, and we'll try straight away?"

"On my way."

I'm surprised to find myself nervous as I punch in the number. I press the loudspeaker button and put the handset on the kitchen table between us. We stare at it warily, as if it's about to explode.

After three rings, a voice answers.

"Hi." He speaks in a hoarse whisper.

"Carl, it's me, Alice. Don't cut the call, please."

There's a long pause. I can hear his breathing, a rasping sound that makes me wonder if he's unwell. "Listen, Jason doesn't know I'm calling you. I'm here with his mum. We want to help you. Can we meet?"

There's a deep groan. "What? Why are you getting Dawn involved? She doesn't need—"

Dawn says, drily, "I'm here, Carl. You're on speakerphone."

"Dawn, don't get caught up in this. It's between me and Jason. He should never have said anything."

"All we want is to help you."

"Nobody can help me. I've got to do this myself, there's no other way."

I lean forward. "But you're not doing it yourself though, are you? You've got Jason mixed up in it."

Dawn puts a gentle hand on my arm. "Let us try to help you, Carl. Will you meet us?"

"I can't meet you, it's too dangerous. There's nowhere safe — and if they know you've met me they'll be after you, too. Anyway, you can't help."

"Don't do anything stupid, will you, Carl? Let us—"

"No! I'll sort this out my own way. Look — I can't talk any longer. I've got to go. I'm chucking this phone."

"But Carl—"

The line goes dead.

We look at each other, shocked. I grab the phone and press redial, but there's only an engaged signal.

"That's it then," Dawn says, making a hopeless gesture. "We can't help him. Even if we knew how." She looks devastated, her face thin and drawn, the skin on her cheeks almost transparent. "All we can do is hope he gets away with it."

I want to reach out and hug her. She looks broken. "You're right, we have to keep hoping. Listen, I got the address of the guy they're planning to rob, too."

"You did?" Dawn's eyes widen. "How did you manage that?"

"I borrowed Jason's car and checked the sat nav. It was in the list of recently visited places. It didn't take much to work out which one it was."

"Clever you."

I sigh. "Not that it'll do us much good." I ponder for a moment. "Unless we want to stake out the house."

"I can't see what use that would be." It's Dawn's turn to sigh, a long-drawn-out, shaky breath. "But I might have a look at it on the internet. Can you give me the address?"

"Here, I'll write it down for you." I reach for a note-book and pen from the worktop behind me. "It's easy to remember."

"Thanks. Perhaps it'll give me an idea." Dawn's voice wobbles slightly as she gazes at the scribbled note.

"Look — I'm going to keep trying," I say, placing a hand on Dawn's arm. I'm struck by how thin it feels beneath the woollen sleeve. "I'll talk to Jason again today. He knows it's a mad thing to do. And what's he doing it for? Not the money, that's for sure. He won't touch it, even if Carl begs him to take some. Jason is risking getting a criminal record, when he's about as far from a criminal as you can get."

Dawn rises from her chair, her movements slow and stiff. She walks over to the window and stands, staring into the garden, her arms folded across her chest. "If only his father was around."

There's a muffled sob and I realise with a shock that she's crying. I feel dreadful. I should never have brought her into this. I'm by her side in an instant, my arms around her. "Don't, please, Dawn. I shouldn't have involved you, it was stupid of me. Please, try not to get upset. There's still hope, perhaps something will happen to stop it. I'll handcuff Jason to a chair — anything to stop him."

Dawn manages a wobbly smile, wiping tears from fragile cheeks. "Silly of me. Yes, we must keep thinking, try everything. Don't worry about me, dear, you did the right thing to tell me, honestly. Let's have another cup of tea and talk about something else for a while."

By the time I leave, she seems to have recovered her normal cheeriness. But as I hug her goodbye, I'm aware once more of the thinness of her body, the slight wobble in her legs. Dawn seems to have aged ten years in the last week. The stress is really getting to her. And if things go badly for Carl and Jason, I daren't think what the effect on her might be.

CHAPTER 40

They say that for each person, there's only one true love. One person that will always be deepest in your heart, always and forever. A friend, a lover, a parent, a grandparent — it doesn't matter what their relationship is to you — they are The One.

For me, that person is Jason. He is the centre of my world, and always will be, whatever he does. I love him for so many reasons. For his strength of character, his sensitivity, his values. The fact that he shows his emotions without shame, his inability to lie, his vulnerability. His openness and generosity. His innate qualities, if you like — the things that come naturally to him.

Of course, nobody is perfect. Everyone is flawed to a greater or lesser degree. Jason is loyal to a fault, for example, which he's demonstrated many times over Carl. He's easily influenced, too soft, too generous. Stubborn, oh yes.

But for me, these flaws are far outshone by his strengths. I don't believe these things are learned: either the strengths or the weaknesses. I think a person is born with certain characteristics, and they form the essence of that individual. Whatever life throws at him, Jason keeps those qualities intact.

That's why my "One" is Jason.

CHAPTER 41

Jason

He sits in the darkness, the night's chill seeping through his clothes. The car has barely warmed up on the way to the meeting point but he daren't keep the engine running. He's not wearing enough for these temperatures, but his choice was limited. There were only a few dark clothes in the cupboard, so he had to wear what he could find — a black T-shirt and hoodie, dark jeans. Luckily his trainers are black anyway, though they have white soles. He keeps having to remind himself that he won't be seen so it doesn't matter what he's wearing.

He slumps low in the seat in case anyone passes by. It's pretty unlikely, at almost three thirty in the morning. The moonlight makes everything look strange, unreal, colours dampened by a blanket of silver. But at least Carl won't need a torch when he scales the walls.

Jason's stomach growls. He's barely eaten in two days. When he looks at food, he feels the bile rising. Despite the cold, his hands are sweating. He wipes them on his jeans, puts his gloves back on. *Come on, Carl. I can't bear the waiting.* He checks his watch for the hundredth time. Funny how slowly time passes when you're waiting for a big moment. There's been no moment bigger — or more ghastly — in his life, and still he wonders how he got here.

Carl's already late. They've agreed that if Carl is more than fifteen minutes late, Jason will leave, and he finds himself tense with the hope that something has happened.

In his wing mirror, a figure emerges from the darkness. It limps towards the car, a bag in one hand. It looks heavy, banging against one black-clad leg. Jason climbs out of the car to open the boot.

"Christ, that weighs a ton," Carl says, panting, heaving the bag into the space.

Great. He hasn't bothered to sort out what he needs. Well, it's his own funeral. Probably literally.

An image of mourners, a dark coffin flashes into Jason's mind. Carl's mum, weeping . . .

"Where are the plates?" Jason says, as Carl opens the passenger door.

"Shit." He returns to the boot. A few minutes pass as he crouches down to affix the false plates.

The suspense is almost too much for Jason. "Get in, let's go." His voice is harsh. Now that it's started, he wants it finished. Every minute feels like it's taking a year off his life.

In the car, neither of them talks, each living his own nightmare. There's hardly anything on the road, and it takes fourteen minutes to reach their destination. Jason brings the car to a halt at the side of the road. They're only a hundred metres or so from Needham's house. "This is it. I go no further."

"Come on, Jason, my ribs are killing me, I can't carry the stuff that far. Drop me outside, then come back here. It's deserted. No one will see you."

Typical Carl. It's useless objecting, it'll only waste more time. Gritting his teeth, Jason puts the car back into gear and drives around the corner, stopping just short of the gate to Needham's house.

"Go!" he says, popping the boot. He waits a moment while Carl extracts the bag, then Jason turns the car and drives back to the next street with a sense of relief. He keeps his eyes away from the rear-view mirror. He doesn't want to see Carl returning, having failed to get over the wall.

He turns off the engine, pulls his hood over his head and folds his hands into his armpits. There's no way he can rest, he's too keyed up and cold, but if anyone looks, they'll think he's fallen asleep. His mind starts to drift.

But then, a flurry of knocks by his ear — he almost jumps out of his skin. Carl is back, gesticulating wildly for him to open the window.

"I can't do it, Jason — you'll have to come."

"I — What?" Something seems to implode in his chest.

"I can't get over the wall, it's too hard on my own. I need your help — come on!"

As he opens the car door, his heart plummets. There's a certain inevitability about this.

You knew this would happen. You complete and utter fool.

CHAPTER 42

Alice

I wake with a start, cursing. I can't believe I slept, though I'm exhausted. I've been keeping myself awake every night, listening for Jason's footsteps on the stairs, waiting to catch him creeping out in the hope that I can stop him. Tonight I was too far gone, and I fell into a daze of strange, frightening dreams in which dark figures ran through the garden, came into our sitting room, stood in corners on the street.

Something must have woken me — was it Jason? Cursing again, I scramble out of bed and throw a robe around me. I tiptoe across the landing to the spare room. The door's closed. The handle squeaks as I turn it and I pause, listening. But when I push the door open, it's clear he's not there. Even though I was half-expecting it, it's a shock.

I sink onto the bed, my hand on the space where he should be. It's happening, right now, and there's nothing I can do about it. My heart beats painfully in my chest, my mind reels. For a millisecond, I wonder if I should call the police. But I can't do that to Jason. Even if I trusted the cops, I can't do that to the man I love.

My mind flits back to my childhood, after my father went to prison. My mother tried so hard with the police. Every couple of weeks she went to the station to talk to them, to plead with them for my father's sake — she was so convinced he was innocent. Sometimes we went with her on the way home from school, and we heard snatches of her conversation at the desk.

"But the evidence is there," she'd say, her voice rising in anger. "Why can't you see it? Just ask him, just question him about it." I didn't know what she was talking about at the time, but I know she thought the Nevilles were to blame. The police were dismissive, even contemptuous. She'd leave the station furious, muttering all the way home. In the end they told her she was being a nuisance and threatened to arrest her if she carried on.

Sometimes we eavesdropped when she called her sister. She'd close the kitchen door, but we were there, our ears glued to the painted wood, and we caught some of what she said. That's how we learned how long he'd be away.

"Five years!" she said one day, her voice thick with emotion. "Five years, and that Jack Neville got nothing! It's all wrong, so unfair . . ."

Then, "My husband has the evidence! I've told them a thousand times . . . I reckon they were bribed. Either that or they were just too lazy to bother. They wanted to charge someone, and it didn't matter who. They picked on him and they wouldn't listen to his side of it.

"He made a stupid mistake, but he was led to it by that — *criminal* — and his evil family . . . he doesn't deserve it."

Tonight, on my own in the empty house, I feel as if history is repeating itself. Jason's the one being pushed into committing a crime, and he'll go down for it.

If he does, I'm going to make damn sure Carl does too.

CHAPTER 43

Jason

He shivers as he waits by the wall for Carl to untangle the ropes and rigging. It's not the temperature making his limbs shake. A toxic mixture of anger and fear courses through his veins. Carl has betrayed him once again. He hasn't even tried — it's clear he gave up before he even got the equipment out of the bag. He is unbelievable.

But there's no point arguing now.

Jason checks the street uneasily. There's no sound, no movement, but they need to be faster than this. He wonders if Carl has even checked for CCTV. He raises his eyes to the telegraph posts and streetlamps. He can't see any sign of cameras — but that doesn't mean there aren't any. Cursing under his breath, he pulls his hood further over his face. Carl has a balaclava over his, so he's better protected. This wasn't what was meant to happen.

At last Carl signals that he's ready. He flings a rope over the wall and pulls until it catches.

"Up you go," Carl says, looking over his shoulder.

"I'm not going over — you go."

"You must. How am I going to get up to the roof without help? You have to come."

Anger rises in Jason's chest. He wants to scream — or better, knock some sense into Carl. But this isn't the time. "You bastard, Carl. Go — just get over the wall, now! Whistle when you're over. I'll bring the bag."

For a moment Carl looks as if he's going to argue, then he nods and climbs upwards, his thin legs flailing before he gets a grip.

Jason waits for his low whistle, then scrambles up the wall, the bag on his back, barely pausing before sliding down the rope to the soft ground on the other side. They hide the rope and crouch, silent, listening. It seems like an age before Carl nods. He leads the way, keeping low, across the drive to the front of the house. He flattens himself against the porch wall. Jason does the same.

"This is the tricky part," Carl whispers, indicating the roof with his eyes. The porch rises up to the second floor where a small decorative parapet offers a handhold. To Jason it looks unreachable, an enormous distance for them to scale. Carl takes the rope, attaches a hook to one end and loops it over his arm. He swings wildly, the rope flying upwards. Twice it fails to catch, landing on the ground at their feet with a thump that sounds like a drum roll to Jason's over-sensitised ears. But at last it holds. Carl adds some metal attachments to a harness and climbs into it. He heads upwards, his feet landing in great strides on the wall. Jason holds the rope steady from the ground. When Carl disappears over the rim of the porch, Jason attaches himself, flinching at the clinking noises. Saying a silent prayer, he hitches himself upwards.

On the roof of the porch, he's relieved to see they're not overlooked by houses opposite or on either side. Tall trees surround them, shielding them from view. Jason can only hope they don't conceal cameras: Needham watching, preparing to spring on them.

Carl wrestles with a window, his screwdriver glinting in the moonlight. The window lock gives way, a tiny metallic crack echoing into the darkness. They freeze beneath the window, hearts thumping. Two minutes pass, then three. There's no sound from within. They breathe again.

"It's okay." Carl removes the lock, placing it carefully on the sill with the screwdriver. He opens the window slowly, checking the dark space inside. "Follow me."

"No. You're on your own now." Jason squats in the shadow of the parapet. "I go no further. Go on, get on with it. I'll wait."

"But—"

"But nothing. I'm done — I'm not going in. Go!"

After a moment of hesitation, his face working through anger to resignation, Carl peers through the open casement into the shadows. He lifts a leg over the windowsill. His body shuffles after it and he's gone.

Moonlight seeps through high cloud, dappling silver on the roof. Crouched in the shadows, waiting, Jason feels strangely alone. He looks out over the garden. Everything is still: no movement, not even a breath of wind.

Only a couple of minutes have passed since Carl crept into the house, but it feels like an hour. All Jason's doubts return. What is he doing here? Why did he let Carl persuade him into this? He's never done anything like this in his life before. The sweat breaks out on his hands, his forehead.

Alice . . . she will never forgive him.

A black-gloved hand on the lintel — his heart leaps from his chest. Carl scrambles over the sill and grabs the window lock, almost dropping the screwdriver in his haste. It takes a moment to replace the lock and push the window closed.

But something's wrong. He's empty-handed, the pack on his back still flat, unopened. Bile rises in Jason's throat.

"Go — go!" Carl gestures wildly towards the edge of the roof, his face contorted, manic.

"Carl, slow down! What's going on — where's the money?"

"Gone. The money's gone, Jason — and Graham's dead."

"What?"

"Just go!" Carl pulls Jason towards the edge. "There's a fucking dead body in there!"

They go. Within seconds they're on the ground, running, running . . .

CHAPTER 44

Jason

He can't stop shaking. Driving away, the two men are struck
dumb, the air in the car full of words unsaid, questions unan-
swered. Jason can barely speak, let alone look at Carl. This is
a catastrophe — worse than he ever imagined. A dead body!
What does that make them? Suspects in a burglary is one thing,
but to be suspected of murder? It doesn't bear thinking about.

As soon as they're well out of the area, Jason stops the
car. He turns off the engine. They sit, stunned, for a moment
before Carl turns to open the door.

He's leaving, just like that, without a word.

"Carl — wait — tell me what happened! How come
Graham's dead?"

"No idea." The door's open, Carl's foot on the pavement.

"But — wait! You—"

"I'm off." Carl cuts him off, his mouth set in a grim line.
"Getting out of here, ASAP. You should too."

"But — where are you going? Shouldn't we talk about
this?" He can't think straight. One thing is certain — this
isn't the end of it. Not with a dead body in a house Carl's
just broken into.

"Nope. We failed. I'm going. Don't try to find me."
The door closes.

"Wait!" Jason calls after him through the half-open window. "The ropes, the kit — take it with you!"

But he's gone, half-running in a strange, limping shuffle down the street.

Jason doesn't stop to see him go. With shaking fingers, he starts the car. All he can think of is getting away. What an unholy mess. Everything's gone horribly wrong — and to top it all, he has a bag of stolen climbing gear in the boot of his car. He must get rid of it — right now.

Though it feels excruciatingly slow, he drives within the speed limit, searching for somewhere to dump it. In a small, run-down industrial park he spots a line of big green bins, the type with sliding lids. Choosing one at random, he throws the bag in. It lands with a deafening clunk.

When he gets back, he parks the car in a side street and removes the false plates with shaking hands. Further down the street, he dumps them at the bottom of a bin, making sure they're out of sight.

He creeps into the house in the dark, trying not to make a sound. In the kitchen, he pours himself a large whisky, a drink he doesn't even like, and waits for his body to calm down. His heart is pounding, his throat so dry he can barely swallow, and the shaking doesn't seem to be about to stop. A million questions hammer at him. What on earth just happened? How come Needham was dead? Where's the money?

What the hell is he going to tell Alice?

All night he stays downstairs, unable to rest, the questions in his mind unrelenting. By daybreak, he feels beaten, every joint in his body complaining. But the last thing he wants to do is face Alice right now.

There's no movement from upstairs as he leaves the house and heads back to the car. He must behave normally, go to work as usual, try somehow to get through the day. In the car he listens to the news, waiting for the local report. No mention of an unexplained death. Either the body hasn't been found yet, or the police are keeping it quiet while they investigate. Or perhaps something else. He's too tired to think it through.

But is he making things worse by doing nothing? Perhaps, now that Carl has deserted him, he should go to the police. He'll be found guilty of aiding and abetting an intended burglary, but that doesn't matter — he'll confess to that, of course. But what if they think he played a part in Needham's death? He has no idea what happened, where the body lay, what it looked like, and what Carl's reaction was, except that he ran. He can only hope he didn't touch him or leave any traces of DNA in the house. They should have reported the body, right then — how can he do it now? If Carl's caught, there's no knowing what he might say. He could implicate Jason in the planning, lie through his teeth to save his skin.

He braces himself. Right now, there are no answers to all these questions. If he carries on agonising over what might happen, he'll go out of his mind. He'll go to work, do his best not to think about last night. Keep checking the news and work out what to do later.

CHAPTER 45

Alice

When I wake up, I'm not even sure if Jason has been back. The bed in the spare room looks unused, his jacket's not in its usual place in the hall. But in the kitchen there's a used glass tumbler, one that rarely comes out of the cupboard. I sniff, flinching. Whisky. Why would Jason be drinking whisky? He doesn't even like the stuff. Now I have a very bad feeling about last night.

I flip my laptop open, check on the news website.

"A man has been found dead at his home near Wimbledon. A local builder, Graham Needham, 73, was found dead this morning by his cleaner . . ."

Dead? How can he be dead?

My hands fly to my face in horror, my stomach falling away. Bile floods my mouth and for a moment I think I'm going to throw up, right there at the kitchen table. The report goes on: *"It's unclear yet as to how he died."*

Please, God, let this have happened before Carl went in.

My eyes are glued to my laptop. Police tape across the gate to the house, patrol cars in the driveway. Not much detail on what they've found. They'll be inside, looking for evidence of all sorts. DNA, broken windows, damaged door frames. If they find anything suspicious, Carl — Jason too, oh my God — will be in worse trouble than I could possibly have imagined.

I dial Jason's number again and again, listening in frustration to the voicemail message click in. "Dammit, Jason, pick up, pick up," I say out loud. I text, my fingers flying. *Are you OK? Please call me.* I daren't say more, in case the police can track messages. If they suspect foul play, there could be a murder investigation.

Murder! The more I think about it, the worse it sounds. My hands begin to tremble now and I fold them into my armpits, rocking backwards and forwards in the chair.

Finally, I force myself to calm down, taking deep breaths. Panicking is not going to help, I tell myself sternly. But I must find out what happened.

Dawn's number flashes on my phone. "Did you hear the news?" she says without preamble. "That man, in the house they were going to rob — he's been found dead."

My heart hits the floor. "You saw it, then. But Dawn, this is terrible. I think they went in last night — Jason went out after I'd gone to bed. They must have decided to go for it."

"Have you spoken to him?"

"No, I can't get hold of him."

"That's not unusual when he's at work, is it?"

"No — but how did Needham end up dead? You don't think—" I can't bring myself to say the words.

"No, I don't. Though I didn't know they were going in last night." Dawn sounds so calm, I'm confused for a moment. I was dreading telling her, aware of the possible implications. But I underestimated her.

"Neither did I."

"Probably a heart attack or something," Dawn continues. "He was in his seventies, wasn't he?"

"Do you think he died before they got there?"

"Let's hope so."

"I'm worried, Dawn."

"We'll know soon enough." Dawn sounds sleepy, her words slurring slightly.

"Are you okay? You sound a bit . . . down."

"I'm fine. Maybe a bit tired, you know. Nothing a rest won't sort out. Call me when you've spoken to him, won't you?"

"Of course. Want me to come over later? I could make you some supper."

"That's kind. But I need a quiet day today. I'll probably go to bed early. We'll talk tomorrow, when you know a bit more."

I cut the call, more worried about Dawn than before. I check my messages. One from Jason — my heart almost leaps from my chest. *I'm OK. Carl's gone. Let's talk later.*

I'm relieved, if Carl really has gone. But I'm not reassured. What on earth happened at the house? I'm both impatient to hear and terrified of what I might learn.

CHAPTER 46

At first I laughed at myself, dismissed it as another crazy idea. But somehow, it stayed with me, and I let it grow, the details working themselves through as if it wasn't my brain doing it, but someone else's. It wasn't long before I started to think it was possible. It could be done, and I was the ideal person to do it.

I was better, cleverer, than both Carl and Jason. I could outsmart them easily — and neither of them would ever suspect me. I knew how to research, understood how to discover all sorts of things on the internet. With a few hours' work and some dogged determination, I found what I needed. I made lists, worked out a timeline, ran through all the possible permutations of my plan. There were unknowns, of course, but I worked on those, too, and thought through all the ways I could handle the different scenarios.

I was fairly confident in myself. When I decide to do something, I do it properly and I see it through. It was risky, for sure, but what Carl was planning — or rather, failing to plan — seemed far riskier. Was I putting myself in any danger? Yes, but nothing I couldn't handle. Was I putting anyone else in danger, as Carl was? No. I liked the neatness of my plan, the way it sidestepped everything, and I was ready to do it.

All that was missing was when they were going to go in — the day and the time — and I was going to find that out, whatever it took.

CHAPTER 47

Alice

He looks like a teenager on his first date. He's white as a sheet and the hand that pushes back the lock of hair from his forehead shakes. I'm pretty sure I look just as bad.

This is going to be tough. I want him to be truthful, to tell me everything that happened. I might not like it at all, but I must know.

"Alice." The expression on his face tells me to brace myself.

"God, Jason, what happened?" The words pour out of my mouth. "I know he's dead, it was on the news. Was it Carl? Did you go?"

Jason makes a hopeless gesture with his hand. "Alice, can we . . . please, sit down? I'm going to tell you everything, I promise."

I don't want to sit, I don't want the niceties — I can't bear the suspense. "Please, Jason — I need to know what's going on. Where's Carl?"

"Honestly, I don't know. He took off."

I open my mouth to reply but he stops me with a gesture. "I'll tell you all of it — I will. But before I do, please believe me — I'm so, so sorry, about everything. You were right. I should have let Carl sort his own mess out. Now everything's gone horribly wrong."

My chest contracts. I can barely breathe. "Tell me."

He hangs his head, his face tortured, and he tells me. I sit there frozen, listening.

"Then — oh God, Alice — he told me to get out of there. He said — he said . . . there was no money, nothing there. And there was . . ." He swallows. "There was — a dead body inside."

I gasp — I can't help it. There's a whining in my ears and I think I might faint. I close my eyes until the feeling passes. When I open them, he's sitting there with his head in his hands. I know he's weeping.

"My God, Jason."

Tears trail down his cheeks. He wipes them away with shaking fingers. "I'm sorry, Alice, I can't tell you how sorry. You knew all along it would be a disaster. Now it's a bloody catastrophe, and Carl's gone. What am I going to do?"

I shake my head from side to side. "I–I honestly don't know what to say."

"I have absolutely no idea how it happened, please believe me. I don't know where the money is, I don't know if Needham was murdered or died of natural causes — I don't even know what Carl did in that house before he came running out."

"What a horrible mess." It's an understatement, but I can't think of another way to describe it.

"I suppose . . . my only defence is that I was trying to help a friend. That's all it was, Alice, please believe me. I'm not a criminal. I would never have agreed to do this if he hadn't been in such a desperate state."

I look up at him then, tears gathering. "I know, Jason. I know you were only trying to help."

"I promise, if only I could go back in time, I would. When I heard what he was planning, I should have refused to listen, stuck to my guns. I'm weak, and I deserve to be in this mess."

146

"No, Jason! Your friend betrayed you. You're not weak. You're too loyal for your own good."

"Not anymore, I promise you. He's gone, and I won't have anything to do with him, ever again."

None of this is Jason's fault, and my heart goes out to him. If misplaced loyalty is Jason's biggest weakness, it doesn't make him a bad person. All I want to do right now is comfort him, help him find a way through all this.

"I don't know what to do, Alice, what am I going to do?" Jason turns pleading eyes to mine. "Carl's gone. I could be in the frame for murder — and the gang's still after us. It couldn't be worse."

I try to think clearly, but my mind's numb with shock. "I don't know what we can do, Jason. But I'm not going to leave you to deal with this on your own."

That's when he starts to sob.

CHAPTER 48

Alice

I stare into the cold light of a grey morning. After falling asleep in the early hours, exhausted, I woke again not long after, my mind unable to rest. I've been gazing at the ceiling ever since, watching as the blackness turns into patchy shadow, then into the flat light of dawn.

I've looked at Jason's situation every which way but it's hopeless. Utterly hopeless.

I head for the shower, closing my eyes as the water streams over my face. Perhaps the only answer is for him to go to the police. If he goes now, today, explains everything and leaves nothing out, it's possible he'll get away with a suspended sentence. But the fact remains, he was an accessory to a crime. A reluctant one, but the police won't care about that — he still knew a crime was about to be committed, and he helped the perpetrator. He agreed only to drive Carl to Needham's house, but he ended up helping him onto the premises. The fact that he didn't go into the house means nothing. He was there, he knew what Carl was planning.

But what about Needham? It might turn out to be a heart attack, or a stroke, or something else to allay suspicions.

If that's the case, Jason needn't go to the police at all. There won't be any questions regarding Needham's death and Jason will be in the clear.

Unless they know about the money. But how would they find out?

They could have found the broken window lock, though Jason says Carl screwed it back into place well. If there's no evidence of anything having been taken, they would probably note the dodgy window lock but take no action. Or — and this gives her another jolt when it occurs to her — it could be obvious that the safe had been tampered with. It might even have been left wide open. Without Carl, they don't know.

If Needham was murdered, what then? Someone could have been in the house ahead of Carl — someone who meant to kill Needham, or killed him while stealing the money. If the police find Carl's DNA or fingerprints, he'll surely be implicated.

Or maybe Carl killed him in self-defence? But in either case, there would be evidence: perhaps a wound on the back of the head, bruises round Needham's neck where he was strangled. A knife wound, blood everywhere. There's been no mention of anything pointing to murder, but that means nothing. The police could be keeping quiet about it while they investigate.

All this agonising is getting me nowhere. I need to know the worst — the penalties for breaking and entering, or trespassing, or driving a perpetrator to the scene of a crime. Accessory to burglary — to a murder. At least I might get some idea of what Jason could get if he decides to hand himself in. Delaying telling the police has almost certainly made things worse, but at least he'll have gone to talk to them willingly.

If he doesn't go to the police, Jason will wonder every single day if he's going to be arrested. He'll be living as if he's a criminal, whichever way you look at it. In one direction are the police, in the other, a dangerous criminal gang.

As I close the front door quietly behind me, I know what I'm going to advise Jason to do. I'll talk to him tonight.

CHAPTER 49

I made myself look very ordinary. I wore scruffy jeans, my oldest jacket. A scarf round my neck, a gardening hat with a floppy brim. Carrying a walking stick and a small backpack, I took the tube to Wimbledon and found the street. There, I made my way slowly along the pavement, limping slightly. Outside the house, I pretended to have a long conversation on my mobile. That way I could study it through the gates without looking too suspicious.

It was easy to spot the CCTV. In the street, there were two cameras facing away from the house — they weren't going to bother me. I could avoid them simply by approaching from the other end of the street. There was another I couldn't avoid, and I could see one attached to the front of the house. No doubt there were more, but I'd have to wait until I was in the garden to check on those. I'd already found a simple way to disable security cameras. I looked it up online. It was so simple, I could hardly believe it — a powerful LED flashlight can disable a camera without the person being seen.

There was no time to mess about.

It was a quiet street with a line of cars parked on one side, double yellow lines on the other. Residents' parking notices were displayed on the lampposts. Of the vehicles coming and going in the street, most were delivery vans, pulling up where they could, leaving their engines running while they delivered their packages. I had to take my chances, and when

I saw a uniformed man approaching the gates of Needham's house, I knew my luck was in. Now I didn't have to think up a lame excuse to get through the gates. I waited until he pressed the buzzer and said: "Delivery" into the intercom.

A man's voice replied: "Leave it on the step by the back door — left side of the house."

I stood behind the delivery man, making sure I wasn't in view of the camera on the entry phone. "I'm going in there," I said.

He turned, startled.

"I'll take it in for you if you like."

He smiled. "Great — thanks. I'm on a tight schedule today. Cheers."

The gate opened slowly as he trotted back to his waiting van. I ducked past the camera on the gatepost and, head down, walked to the side of the house, where I left the package on the step as instructed. Without pausing, I checked the back door — a Yale lock and a more robust Chubb. Of course, there could be bolts on the inside, but I could do nothing about them. If there were, and he used them at night, I'd have to find another way in.

I walked back towards the front of the house, but instead of heading for the gate, I stepped quickly off the path into the bushes to the left where wood chippings provided a dry cushion to sit on. With my back against the wall, I had a clear view of the side door and the front drive. I made myself comfortable as the gate clicked shut.

Now all I had to do was wait and hope.

CHAPTER 50

Jason

The sharp tones of his phone penetrate a deep, dreamless sleep. Coming out of it is a struggle, registering the present even harder in the fraction of a second it takes to hit the answer button.

The number is unknown. This could be it: the dreaded call from the police. His stomach churns.

"Hello?"

"Jason, this is your mum's friend, Hilary."

It takes him a moment to register who she is, his mind occupied with uniforms and squad cars. "Ah, yes, Hilary. How are you?"

"I'm fine. But your mum's taken a turn for the worse, I'm afraid. She collapsed this morning and she's been taken to hospital."

He turns the words over but doesn't seem to recognise them. "A-a turn for the worse?"

There's a pause at the other end of the line. "Ah. I wondered if she'd told you. I think it's better you hear it from her, or her doctor. But you need to go and see her. Have you got a pen?" Hilary has always been a woman of few words.

He writes down the name of the ward in a daze.

"How — how is she? Is she conscious?"

"Oh yes, she is. I called a few minutes ago. She seems to be what they call 'comfortable'."

"I — thank you, Hilary. I'll get there as soon as I can."

He dresses in a rush, not caring what he looks like. What has his mum been hiding from him, and for how long? It must be serious for her to collapse and be taken to hospital. Alice noticed, but he should have seen it himself — she shouldn't have needed to point out to him that his mother wasn't right. Without even thinking to check the street, he races to the tube station, his mind on one thing only. Nothing else matters right now.

The nurse points to a bed in the corner of a small room, curtains drawn around it. "She's sleeping now — it's best not to wake her. But you can stay as long as you like."

His mum sleeps peacefully, her hands folded across her chest, the skin on her face and arms a deathly white, save only for a scattering of freckles on the backs of her hands. Only the slight rise and fall of her chest indicates that she's alive. They've put a hospital gown on her and a drip in one thin arm, attached to a bag hanging from a contraption above her head.

He draws a chair to the bedside, taking care not to make a noise, and waits.

After a while another nurse puts her head around the curtain, startling him. "Hello," she says in a low voice. "Are you a relative?"

"I'm her son."

"I need to do her blood pressure, so she might wake up now."

"Uh, before you do that, can you tell me what it is? Why did she pass out? Does she have something I don't know about?"

"Let me see if I can find the doctor. It's best you talk to her."

In a few moments the nurse returns. She beckons and they leave the bedside. Jason follows her a short distance to

153

an empty waiting area. She indicates a chair in the corner. "The doctor will be with you shortly."

The doctor is a small Asian woman with graceful hands and kind eyes. She sits next to him. "You're Mrs Green's son."

"Yes — Jason. Can you tell me what's wrong? I didn't even know she was ill."

"This is a cancer ward," the doctor says gently. "I'm sorry."

He closes his eyes. How did he not know that? He didn't even register where he was in the hospital. What a stupid, thoughtless fool he is.

He clears his throat, but he can barely speak. "What — what kind of cancer is it?"

"It's a rare form of lung cancer." She says its name, but he hears nothing over the sound of rushing in his ears. "She's been seeing an oncologist for a month or so."

"She's known for a month?"

"It seems she knew for quite a while before she saw her GP, but did nothing about it. A friend pushed her into getting checked." She hesitates. "I'm afraid it's quite advanced — I'm so sorry."

It's like he's fallen into the deepest, darkest abyss. "What . . . I — What can you do for her?" he stammers. "Is she having chemotherapy?"

The doctor hesitates. "When she got the initial test results, she took the decision not to have chemotherapy."

He swallows. "Why? Why didn't she want it?"

"Well . . . unfortunately, it would only lengthen her life by a few weeks, at best. It wouldn't cure her condition — the cancer has advanced too far — and it would make her quite poorly. When she heard that, she said she didn't want to go through all the side effects in the time she has left. She wants to be alert for as long as possible. We're offering palliative care now."

"What does that mean, exactly? Do you mean . . . ?"

"I'm so sorry. She has a few weeks, possibly two months, at best."

CHAPTER 51

Jason

"A few weeks? But—" A painful thud starts up in his forehead. That's not possible. "She's . . . She was . . ."

He's stunned into silence. Only two months ago, his mum was fit and healthy, enjoying her classes, walking, shopping — even going dancing. It was hard to find a day when she wasn't busy. This has happened so fast — too fast. The thudding in his head grows stronger.

"It is a particularly aggressive form of cancer — it moves quickly," the doctor says. "When she first came to see us, it had already spread to other parts of her body. She seemed to know already that the prognosis wouldn't be positive. She accepted it straight away."

That figures. His mother was never one to complain. She wouldn't want a drama, even over something as serious as this. Numb with shock, he struggles to find the words.

"And — and there's really nothing you can do?"

The doctor's eyes are full of sympathy. "Nothing, I'm afraid. Even if she agreed to chemotherapy, it would make very little difference to her life expectancy — and there are unpleasant side effects. She's in no pain at the moment.

Palliative care is very sophisticated these days; there's no need for her to suffer unnecessarily. We'll keep her comfortable for as long as possible." She looks over her shoulder towards the bed where Dawn lies. "I think the nurse has finished now, if you're ready to go back. I'm sure she'll be happy to see you."

"Thank you. And thank you for being honest with me. Could I–I need a few minutes before I see her."

"Of course. I'll ask someone to get you some tea, if you'd like?"

"That would be very kind, thank you."

He sits in the empty waiting area for a few moments, his emotions churning, tears pricking at his eyelids. He doesn't want his mother to see him like this — she would hate to be the cause of grief. But the ground has moved under his feet, and his life will never be the same. Just like that, with a single phone call, a short conversation. She'll be gone by Christmas. He'd never even thought about it, her death. He'd taken it for granted that she'd be around for years, decades to come. This is far too soon. It doesn't seem possible.

It's so unfair.

* * *

"Hi, Mum." He steps through the curtains. "Can I come in?"

Her eyes are open, though there's a sleepy look about her. "Jason, dear. Of course, sit down. Sorry to drag you away from work — I hope it wasn't a problem. I said not to bother you, but Hilary insisted."

He takes her hand in his. "She was right to insist — it's not a problem, not at all. Of course I would want to come and see you."

Her eyes search his, and he hopes she can't see the red rims around them.

"It's okay, Mum. I've had a chat with the doctor and she's told me everything. I'm — I'm going to look after you." Her hand is cool and thin, purple veins patterning the skin like rivers on a map. The sight of it is deeply saddening. His own skin is smooth and plump by comparison.

"Everyone has to go sometime, don't they?"

Tears threaten again and he swallows, hard. "But not everyone goes so soon, Mum."

She sighs, a deep, trembling sound, and he imagines the intruder in her lungs. "I've had a full life, though, haven't I? And the best thing in it is you."

He is too choked to speak.

She strokes his hand, comforting him as she's always done. "Now tell me about you and Alice. I want to know you'll be okay. You can be really happy with her — I know it."

He tries to smile, though it probably looks like a grimace. "You're right, Mum, and it's all fine — we're back together. Carl's gone. I've promised Alice I'll have nothing to do with him if he comes back. There are things I need to do to make amends — to make it up to her — but it'll be okay."

She smiles, her sigh touching his hair. "Thank goodness. That makes me happy. Hang on to her now, won't you?"

"I sure will."

"But what's this about Carl? Have you fallen out?"

"It's a long story, Mum. I'm not going to bother you with the details, but he let me down again — badly this time. He did something . . . unforgivable. It's not what friends do to each other. Alice is furious with him, and she's right to be. Luckily, he's legged it."

"Where to?"

"I have no idea. And I don't want to know. He's left me with a bit of a mess to sort out — don't worry, nothing serious." For once he forgives himself for telling a white lie to his mother. "Nothing I can't manage."

She relaxes back into her pillows, her hand still in his.

"How are you feeling now, Mum?"

"A lot better, thank you. A bit tired. I'll have a sleep later, I'll be fine."

"Anything I can bring you? I'll be here for you, whenever you need me."

"No, really, I'm fine. They're looking after me very well. All I need is some rest. The doctor says I can go home in a few days, once they've done all the tests. But they say I'll have to get some care." A worried look passes across her face.

"That's great, Mum — you'll be better at home. Don't worry about anything, I'll sort it all out, I promise. Alice will help too — I know she'll want to."

Nothing else matters now, only his mum.

CHAPTER 52

Alice

This changes everything. I was expecting to have a long discussion with Jason about going to the police, and the implications of that. There's no way I can do that now. Though I'm deeply upset by the news, my mind is clear on this. Jason can't risk losing the short time he has left with Dawn. He mustn't go to the police — he can't be implicated.

I must do all I can to protect him now.

There are two things we can hope for. First, and most important, that Needham died of natural causes, removing the possibility of a murder rap. Carl might be the only person who can tell us that right now, until the post-mortem is done. The second is that the police don't find out about the money. I wouldn't take a bet on either of them.

I call my boss, tell her about Dawn, and ask for a couple of days off. I'm owed some holiday days and it's a quiet time of year for us, so it's not a problem.

The doorbell goes as I disconnect the call. I check from the sitting room window, as I've started to do in the last weeks. Julie spots me, gives a quick wave. She's holding flowers and a cake tin.

"Hi, Julie, how nice to see you."

"Alice, I wanted to tell Jason . . . I—I was so terribly sad to hear about his mum."

"Thanks, Julie. Jason's not here right now, he's at the hospital. But come in anyway."

Julie follows Alice to the kitchen. "I brought these for Jason to take to Dawn." She hands over the flowers and the cake tin. "How's he doing?"

"He's holding up, though it's hard. She'll be home soon, but she's going to need nursing care." My voice wobbles. I can't talk about it without tears in my eyes. "They're not treating her for the cancer now, only with pain relief. But she seems comfortable."

"I'm glad she can go home. Hospitals are terrible places to spend the last days of your life."

"Indeed. Listen, Julie, I'm glad you came over. Have you heard from Carl at all?"

"I was wondering if you had, actually. I had a text from him a couple of days ago, from a strange phone number. I suppose he ditched his mobile. Anyway, he was in Spain, but he said he was moving on. Is he still in trouble?"

I hesitate. "To be honest, I don't know. But I think it's the right thing for him to lie low, at least for a while. Those were bad guys he got tangled up with."

"I asked him to let me know where he is, but maybe it's dangerous to keep in touch."

"He'll contact you when he feels safe, I'm sure of it." I hesitate. I don't want to alarm Julie. "You haven't seen that suspicious car again, have you? Or anything like it — men hanging about the street, any calls for Carl?"

"Nothing in particular. It seems a strange thing to say, but I'm hoping they think he's dead. Or at least, still in hospital where they can't touch him."

"That's possible. We've seen nothing of them either, so you could be right."

Though I'm doing my best to reassure Julie, I have a horrible feeling we're all being naive. A criminal gang, owed a lot of money, would surely not give up this easily. Especially if it's the Nevilles — their reputation is well-known. It's possible the police have found them, or frightened them off, at least for the moment, but I'm not convinced.

"Julie, would you do me a favour? I can't check with the police to see if they're any closer to finding Carl's attacker, as I'm not family. They'd talk to you, though. Would you ask them, and let me know what's happening? We'd feel much safer if they track those guys down and put them away. They know where we live, too."

"Of course. I'd like to know myself. I'll call them today."

"Thanks, Julie. And try not to worry."

"I can't help it — I'm his mum, it's in my hormones."

"Of course it is. But Carl's a survivor — he'll find his way."

"I hope you're right. It's true, ducking and diving comes naturally to him. He gets it from his dad."

I feel a prickle of curiosity. "Is his dad still around? I'm being nosy, you don't need to tell me if you don't want to."

Julie sighs. "He's still in London, yes — though we don't see him. He's a builder. Done well for himself. Not that we see any of it."

"Has Carl met him, then? Jason says he never talks about him."

"He did some work for him a while back, actually."

"Did he? So he knows his father?"

"He knows him, but he doesn't know he's his dad. I told Carl he was an old family friend. Carl's never wanted to find his dad — he's always been adamant about that. His decision, and I respect that."

"Then how …?"

"I got him the job. I kind of regret it now, it probably would have been better for them never to have met. But at the time — well, I thought it was the least the bastard could do: give the son he abandoned some work. Carl was out of a job and kicking his heels, getting up to all sorts, and I was still supporting him on my own. It worked well for a while."

She sighs. "Until they fell out. I wasn't surprised, to tell you the truth."

I flinch. It's as if someone has hit me over the head. Surely not. No, it couldn't be. Could it?

"Alice? Are you okay?"

"I — yes, I'm fine. Sorry — just . . ." I try to order my thoughts. "So Jackson's not his father's name then?"

"It's mine. We weren't married. Carl was an accident — in a good way, you know — he's my son, and I love him, despite all his faults. No, his dad's name is Needham. Graham Needham."

CHAPTER 53

Alice

I freeze.

"What is it, Alice? You look like you've seen a ghost." Julie puts a hand on my arm, a look of concern in her eyes.

I hesitate, but only for a moment. She'll find out soon anyway — and it sounds like she won't be too upset at the news.

"I'm fine, Julie, but this is . . . a bit of a coincidence. Hold on, let me find something for you." I open the laptop that's sitting on the worktop, locate a browser. A few moments later I have it. I turn the screen for her to see.

It's her turn to widen her eyes. "My goodness, I see what you mean," she says, reading rapidly. "Wow. That is a bit of a coincidence, isn't it?" She reads it all again, nodding. "So the old bastard's dead. Well, he never did take much care of himself. Too much booze, too many chips. It takes its toll."

"I'm sorry, Julie. But I thought . . . better you know, isn't it?"

She waves a hand. "Oh, don't worry about me, I barely knew him — and he did nothing for us. I wonder what happened to his wife and kids. I know he got divorced years ago, but I never did find out where they went."

"Will you tell Carl, when you speak to him?"

She thinks for a moment. "Can't see the point, really. If it comes up in conversation, maybe — but I don't think he'll care. What did that man ever do for him? There'll be nothing in the will for us, that's for sure."

A thought occurs to me. "Will you go to the funeral?"

"Why would I do that? I never knew him properly — or his family. No, no point at all. Look at the time — I must get on, Alice. Keep in touch."

"Will do — thanks, Julie." I'm lost in thought as I see her to the door — an idea's been triggered by our conversation. There might be a way to find out what really happened to Needham.

I could go to the funeral.

Under normal circumstances, I'd think the idea was mad. I know that funerals are public, but I doubt many people go to the funeral of a complete stranger. Certainly not people like me. But these are not normal circumstances.

I could discover how he died — it'll be quicker than waiting for the coroner's report. Also, I might learn something about Needham's family — they'll surely emerge, if only in expectation of something in his will. Someone will have to identify the body and organise the funeral — unless they're so estranged they want nothing to do with it. The family could be a threat to Jason's safety, if they know about Needham's stash of money — and if they do, they'll almost certainly suspect foul play if it's disappeared. They may talk about it at the funeral.

I'm not great at pretence. I can't act to save my life, and I worry that I might stick out like a monkey at a tea party. I certainly can't get away with going to the wake, if there is one. But I might just be able to make up a plausible reason for sitting at the back of a funeral, even if I never knew the deceased person. I have to go.

It's weird. This is a world I never thought I'd be in — criminals, post-mortems, gangs, people being beaten up. I know nothing about it and it's terrifying. All I'm doing is trying to stop the man I love being arrested. All I want is a quiet life. Normality.

The realisation dawns on me, like a dark cloud descending, that normality as we knew it might never return.

CHAPTER 54

Alice

There's someone else I have to see, someone who might be able to shed some light. I can travel there and back in a day, without bothering Jason with what I'm doing. He has enough to deal with at the moment.

I catch an early train and I'm there in just over three hours. I don't need long.

These days I see my parents every few months. It's not very often, I know. It's not that I don't love them — but once they moved away from London, Sarah and I wanted nothing more than to get on with our lives and forget the shame of our dad having been in prison. Even though she failed to enrol us in her religious beliefs, I suppose Mum's fervour had an effect on us, because we lived our teenage years fearing the backlash. We were ashamed, and I'm still not proud of the fact that my father has a criminal record. But I don't hold a grudge and I've moved on.

"Hello, doll," my dad says when he opens the door. He always called us "doll" and it still takes me back to when I was a kid. "Hi, Dad," I say, giving him a peck on the cheek.

"Come on in." Dad walks with a bandy-legged sway to the sitting room, where Mum's chintz still dominates — faded and repaired now, it must be at least thirty years old.

"How are you, Dad? Managing your diabetes okay?" Dad lost a lot of weight about a year ago for no apparent reason. Mum finally persuaded him to go to the doctor and diabetes was diagnosed.

"Don't you worry about me. It's a nuisance, but that's all. Your Mum keeps me in line, makes sure I keep taking the tablets. She's at a church meeting. She'll be back soon."

"I know." I'd chosen today because I knew she'd be out all morning. She's like clockwork with her meetings, never misses one. "There's something I wanted to talk to you about though, Dad, before she gets back. Something she won't want to discuss."

We sit on cushions misshapen from years of use, bent into the shapes of bodies gone before. I look around the room. All the same ornaments, pieces of china, knickknacks from my childhood memories. All still there, dust-free. Mum has always been house-proud, even though there's never been much money. A threadbare rug that came from our London house, the same oak sideboard — I can list with perfect accuracy what's kept in there.

"Fire away, love. Glad to talk — don't get much chance with your mum around." He winks, the same old Dad. Still a bit of a rogue, too, I'll bet.

"Dad, I want you to tell me about the Nevilles."

That makes him look — I knew it would. We've never spoken properly about what happened to him, even after Sarah and I grew up. Distance and bad memories came between us.

He sucks his teeth, gives me a sideways look. "You're not in any trouble, are you, doll?"

"No, not me, a friend. The name came up, and it got me wondering. I never asked — and you never said — what really happened with Jack Neville."

He takes a long, slow breath. "You were too young, and then your mum was too upset. She hates to talk about it, even now. The Nevilles, eh?"

I nod.

"Steer clear, is my advice. From what I hear — and I do hear, believe me — they're bigger and badder than they ever were. Not just thieving now, some seriously bad stuff going on in that family. Old Jack's some kind of Godfather now in West London. If he was ruthless then, you can bet he's a hundred times worse now — and the rest of his family."

"What happened with you, though?" I'm keen to get to the bottom of this before Mum gets back.

"I was caught, and Jack Neville wasn't. Simple as that. Your mum never believed I did it, she was a hundred per cent sure I was innocent. But I wasn't, I have to tell you that. I knew what I was doing, and I knew it was a dodgy business. It was his idea, but he didn't force me into it — I was happy to be part of it. We joined forces. We fleeced a lot of people out of a ton of money — tens of thousands of quid, in fact. It was exciting, for a while." He glances over at me, shrugs his shoulders. "I was young and stupid. Wouldn't do it now, your mum got me straightened out. In the end, I got a fair sentence and he got away with it all, including the money." He shakes his head. "He was wily, old Jack, had the coppers in his pocket all the time. I wasn't surprised, to tell you the truth."

"But — I know Mum was convinced you were innocent, Dad — but she also claimed you had evidence against him. She kept on at the police to talk to you about it, to bring him in for questioning. They didn't listen, obviously — but was that true?"

To my surprise, he smiles, then chortles. "Bless her, her heart's in the right place. I'm lucky she stuck with me. It's true, I had evidence against Jack Neville. I wasn't as stupid as he thought. Right from the beginning, I kept it all — the numbers, the bank statements, the transfer notes. Names, addresses, contact numbers. If the police hadn't been bent, Jack would have been caught and put in prison along with me. And a lot of other bad stuff would never have happened, you can bet your life."

"Don't you hate him, though, Dad?" I'm curious. "I'm pretty sure I'd have gone all out to get my revenge."

He laughs, a deep, throaty guffaw. "I wasn't innocent — might have felt differently if I had been. He got away with it, but I'm not angry with him. The cops, though — that's a different matter. Once I realised they were in Jack's pocket, I didn't have a hope. I told them all about Jack, but they wouldn't listen. His name wasn't even mentioned in court. He was a wily one, old Jack."

"Does he know you grassed on him?"

"Pretty sure he would — the cops would've told him."

"Does the name Bennett mean anything to you? Was he one of them? He's a DS now, but he'd have been a uniform then."

"Bennett — no. But I reckon they've all retired now, on their ill-gotten gains."

"Interesting. And Jack didn't come after you?"

"No — why would he? He put me in prison. He was laughing, he didn't need me anymore. I was no more than a piece of shit on his shoe."

"Does he know you have the evidence against him?"

Dad shrugs. "The police knew at the time, but they did nothing about it. Why would they bother to tell him when they knew they weren't going to cop him? It meant nothing to him, even if he did know."

I'm thinking about DS Bennett. My gut feeling tells me he's straight.

"Dad — you wouldn't have kept the evidence, would you? It's just — I'm thinking it might . . . help my friend. It's possible he's got tangled up with the Nevilles."

A look of alarm crosses his face. "Not Jason, I hope?"

"No, not Jason." My dad raises an eyebrow. "Honestly, Dad, it's not Jason. Did you keep it?"

He winks at me, taps the side of his nose with a finger. Slowly he places his other hand on the laptop that sits on the table beside him.

CHAPTER 55

I felt like a different person in my burglar gear. Confident, powerful. I knew what I was doing, and I was cleverer than all of them.

When he came out, I was ready. He was clearly a person of habit — perhaps not a good idea for someone with a huge stash of cash in his upstairs room. He'd become complacent, assuming nobody knew. I watched as he set the alarm and closed the door behind him.

He shuffled off down the drive, his large figure illuminated by the bright security light — the one that was going to be broken by the time he returned. I waited a few minutes before creeping out from the darkness of my hiding place. Now I could check the place out properly.

It was easy enough to deal with the cameras — my stick came in very useful — and with the help of a stepladder, conveniently left in an unlocked shed, the security light was smashed. Within minutes I was done. I waited in the bushes, my eyes on the gate.

When at last he arrived, I was pleased to see how drunk he was. I could just make out his figure stumbling down the drive, his feet shuffling across the gravel. I saw him pause and look up when the light failed to come on, but he shook his head and carried on. It took him a good few seconds and plenty of cursing to get his key into the lock and disable the alarm just inside the doorway.

I crept to the back of the house where I watched him from the shadows beside the sitting room windows. He settled into a chair with a large tumbler in one hand. He flicked through a few channels on the TV until he found the football, increased the volume and settled in for the rest of the evening.

It was time for me to make a move.

CHAPTER 56

Jason

"Take all the time you need, mate," Jason's boss says. "You need to look after your mum. We'll hold the fort, don't worry."

He visits Dawn in hospital every day, sitting beside her bed for an hour or so, reading or talking. Sometimes he watches her face as she sleeps, at other times he holds her hand and talks to her. She nods, saying little, but she seems to like him being there.

He creates a special place in her house. At the back is a small conservatory, facing west, catching the sun from lunchtime onwards, looking out over the small garden. His mum's indoor plants thrive in the warmth and the sunlight on the windowsill. He sets up a bed, angling it into the best position, close to the window but in a shady spot. From there, she'll be able to watch as birds gather on the feeders hanging from the lower branches.

He cleans the entire house, makes up the spare room for the carer, and changes the linen in Dawn's bedroom. Grief and anger give him a brittle energy, and he's glad to be physically active. He finds a flat panel of wood in the shed and

172

fashions a small ramp for the back door, in case she needs a wheelchair to get in. At the supermarket he fills a trolley with food for the freezer and the cupboards, so that all the carer will need to do is buy fresh items. His mum eats like a bird, but the carers will need to eat, too.

Back home, his mind is still full of his mum and all the things he needs to do to look after her. Thoughts of Carl and police, bad guys and dead bodies are far from his mind. So for a moment, he's confused when he makes out the uniform at the front door. But then, with a dizzying thump in the stomach, he remembers.

"Good evening, sir." The officer is young, fresh-faced.

"How can I help you?"

"I believe you made a statement. About Carl Jackson?"

His gut clenches. "Ah yes, I did. Come in."

The officer removes his hat and steps inside. Jason leads him to the kitchen, his heart beating fast. The memory of that disastrous night hurtles back in stomach-churning detail. But he mustn't give himself away. Is this about the break-in? Surely not. They wouldn't send a young officer to the house. They'd want him to come into the station. Wouldn't they? Please let it be about the attack on Carl.

He swallows. "Would you like a coffee? Tea?" His voice sounds all wrong, too polite. Guilty.

"No, sir. This won't take a minute. May I?" He gestures at the table.

"Of course."

The young man sits and retrieves a small notebook from his pocket. He flicks through the pages. The skin on his cheeks is smooth and slightly flushed. Jason wonders if he's nervous. That would make two of them.

"I understand Mr Jackson is a friend of yours?" he says.

Jason's stomach rumbles. He hopes the officer can't hear it — it might be a sign of guilt. "I . . . yes, I've known him since I was a kid."

"He got a pretty serious beating." A statement, not a question.

"Terrible. Did you catch them yet?"

The policeman clears his throat. He checks his notes pointedly. "Has Mr Jackson been in touch with you?"

"We've heard nothing from him, I'm afraid."

"So, you don't know where he is?"

"I have no idea." It's true. If Carl's moved on, he could be anywhere in the world. "I was hoping you might be able to find him."

The young man sighs, closing his notebook. He looks around. "Do you work from home?" he says.

"Ah, no. I've got a few days off. My mum's in hospital."

"Sorry to hear it. Please let us know if you think of anything. You have our number." He stands.

"Wait — has there been any progress? Do you have any leads? My girlfriend's scared, and I am too."

"Our enquiries are ongoing." He hesitates, then seems to relent. "Look, it looks like they've gone to ground for the moment. But please be vigilant — and call us if you see them again, or if anything unusual happens. And if you hear from Mr Jackson. We need to talk to him again."

"Of course."

Once the door is firmly shut behind the policeman, Jason leans his back against it and slides to the floor. He sits there until the thumping of his heart slows.

174

CHAPTER 57

Alice

The crematorium is remarkably quiet from the outside, no knots of people greeting each other before going in, not a single person in sight as I approach. I had hoped to pass unnoticed amid the mourners, arriving just in time, hovering for a few moments until I could slip in at the back.

The building sits in well-tended gardens, a car park behind, a long path leading past clipped grass borders to imposing wooden doors. A pang of uncertainty slows me, my feet pausing on the gravel. I wonder if I've got the wrong day. But I've already checked and double-checked. It's definitely today, and it's due to start in five minutes. Perhaps everyone is already inside.

It was a difficult decision, to come to Needham's funeral. It feels deeply wrong to attend a funeral of someone I don't know, even if my reasons are justifiable. But last night I couldn't get the idea out of my head, and it seemed the only way to short-cut the wait for the coroner's verdict. Without knowing how Needham died, we're living on the edge, dreading what might happen next.

I fill my lungs and push gently on the door. Soft music plays, muffling the sound of my entrance as I slip through and into a seat at the very back of the room, only exhaling once I'm sitting down. I keep my head down, lifting my eyes to look around once I'm settled.

The coffin sits unadorned at the front of the large space, an official-looking person standing nearby, his hands folded. Two figures in black sit straight-backed in the front row — a thin, balding man and a tiny, birdlike woman in a black circular hat. Nobody else is here — all the other seats are empty.

This seems deeply sad. Even if Needham was a fraudster, stealing money from the Inland Revenue — even if he was unpleasant or a loner, to have so few people mourn you when you die is tragic.

As the official starts to speak, the man at the front turns and looks around, his eyes scanning the empty room, eventually landing on me. I shrink into my seat, dropping my gaze to the floor, but I know he must be wondering who I am and why I'm there.

I barely listen as the service drones on, only pricking my ears when the official makes comments about the deceased — but the words are generic, so impersonal they could have been describing anyone. Before I know it, the curtains move to conceal the coffin. It's over in a matter of minutes. The two figures at the front turn to leave by the side door. I follow at a distance.

Outside they're waiting for me. They look like a perfectly ordinary couple, the man uncomfortable in a suit a size too big, the woman in flat, sensible shoes and skirt. I hold back, but the man steps forward with a hint of a smile.

"Are you a friend of Graham's?" he says, holding out a hand.

It's cold and clammy to the touch, and there's no hint of a grip.

"Ah, no. Apologies — are you family?"

He nods. "I'm his brother. Long-lost brother, I should say. Luke. And this is my wife, Mary."

"I'm Alice. I'm afraid I'm here under false pretences really — my mother-in-law hasn't got long to live." That, at least, is true. I've been rehearsing all morning, uncertain of my ability to deceive. "She lives not far from here. I thought it would be empty — I hope you don't mind that I snuck in at the back."

"Ah, I see. Should've known Graham wouldn't have any friends. None that cared enough to come to his funeral, that is. They'll all be down the pub as usual."

I squirm a little inside. "That's sad."

"Yeah, well, he was never one to be sentimental. Always put two fingers up at the world. He didn't even bother to stay in touch with his kids. We can't all be decent and upstanding." A crooked smile crosses his face. His wife nods at his attempt at a joke, taking his arm. We turn and walk together towards the car park.

"Where are his children now, then?"

"There was a pretty acrimonious divorce. His wife took him to the cleaners, apparently. Then she took the children and emigrated to Australia, where she remarried. I don't think Graham ever saw his kids again. Though I doubt if he wanted to — he wasn't a great father." He shrugs. "I suppose it was a miracle anyone married him in the first place."

"Was he unwell, your brother?" I've agonised over how to approach the subject, and this seems the best way to go about it. And probably the only chance I'll have — clearly there isn't going to be a wake.

"Not that we knew. But we weren't in touch, not in the last few years, anyway. He wasn't bothered with family. But he was fat and unfit—" Mary makes a disapproving face. "Well, he was, Mary, he didn't look after himself. I reckon his lifestyle did for him. Probably a heart attack, but we won't know for sure until the coroner's report. He was found by his cleaner, you see, so it was sudden. Nobody was with him when he died."

I frown. "I thought you couldn't get a funeral organised until the coroner's report is done . . . I'm sorry to ask."

"It's true, but they gave us an interim death certificate, which meant we could register the death and go ahead with the cremation."

"I see." No mention of anything suspicious, then. Perhaps the police are satisfied Needham died naturally.

I can only hope.

CHAPTER 58

At home, I'd practised with my own front door, slipping my credit card downwards smoothly to release the lock. I wasn't expert at it, by any means, but I knew it was possible. I also knew that this part could go badly wrong, and I held my breath as I slid the slip of plastic down the doorjamb. The lights in the corridor were off, thankfully, and I held the torch between my teeth as I tried for the third, fourth time to manoeuvre the card into exactly the right spot.

At last it slid downward, releasing the lock. I was triumphant — I'd passed the first test. I stepped into the hall and closed the door behind me, careful not to make a sound.

I slipped through the hallway like a wraith. The living room door was ajar and the shouts of the football crowd followed me as I crept up the stairs. There was no other movement in the house. Needham was either asleep or engrossed in the TV. On the upper floor, all the doors were open bar one. The room with the safe. I was relieved to see it was a normal door, not reinforced, not what you'd expect to find in a proper safe room.

Now was the most difficult part.

I had no idea if Needham's alarm covered this room, or if it was on a separate loop — all I'd got was a code for the safe. It was written on the inside of my wrist.

The door was locked. Undeterred, I took from my pocket the lock-picking tool I'd found online — amazing what you can get online these days — and set to. This, too, I'd spent a long time practising at home. It certainly didn't work every time, but in a short space of time I'd got quite proficient at it. I prayed the lock was similar to mine. But luck was on my side that night. It took a few heart-stopping minutes, but at last it clicked open.

I pushed the door gently, tensing for the sound of an alarm, ready to run. But there was none. I had a quick look around the walls and ceiling, my LED torch ready, but there was no sign of any other security. Perhaps Needham assumed the main alarm, or his presence in the house, were enough to put intruders off.

It doesn't do to assume, Needham.

This was the final hurdle. Bar getting back out undetected, of course.

The room was set up as an office, with filing cabinets along one wall. Opposite was an old-fashioned leather-topped desk and a swivel chair. On the desk was an in-tray with a pile of papers and a closed laptop. The safe, a small, squat metal box with what looked like a brass handle, sat on the floor to one side.

I crouched down and took a look. There was no evidence of any wires attached to it, or any gadget on the exterior, and though my knowledge of security systems was minimal, I was relieved.

I punched in the code.

To my immense surprise, it worked. I was fully expecting it to be wrong — either Carl's mate had been leading him on, or Carl had got the numbers wrong. But the door swung open without a sound. I felt sick when I saw the piles of money in there — wads and wads of it, each pack of notes secured with an elastic band.

I could hardly believe I'd got this far. I was actually going ahead with this. For a moment I hesitated. Every fibre of my being had learned not to do wrong, and this had "wrong" written all over it. But I had to do it, for Jason's sake. It was the rest of his life on the line, and I was going to make sure it wasn't wrecked by Carl.

Sweating, I began to transfer the sheaves of notes into my backpack. I had no idea how much I was taking, but I stuck to the fifty-pound notes and then moved on to the twenties. There was too much for my backpack, but I had to be sure I had enough, so I stuffed it full until the zip would barely shut. For good measure, I filled my jacket pockets, too, and my jeans. I took every last note, and replaced what I'd taken with the contents of the in-tray and a few files I found in the desk drawers. If the police investigated, it would hopefully look — at least at first — as if nothing had been taken.

I closed the safe door, reset the keypad and turned to go, shouldering my now-heavy bag. All I needed to do now was get out of there safely.

I was halfway down the corridor when he appeared.

CHAPTER 59

Jason

"Want me to cut the grass?" Jason gazes out over a garden bathed in sunlight. "I can do it one evening after work, now the days are longer."

"If you don't mind." His mother sits in her favourite armchair, close to the open door, a blanket over her knees. Though the weather's warm for April, there's a chill in the breeze, and she feels the cold very much these days.

She's been home for two weeks now. Though frail and tired, needing to rest every afternoon, she gets up every morning, dresses carefully and goes downstairs, where she spends the day reading or sleeping. A carer comes in to help with her medication and with bathing, cooking and cleaning the house. For the moment she's managing with minimal help, but Jason's under no illusions. Every little thing exhausts her. She has a complicated regime of medication, which helps with the pain but makes her a little confused, and other side effects have meant a number of changes already.

But his mother's made of strong stuff. She likes to get outside every day, sometimes for a stroll round the garden, sometimes to the end of the street and back on the nurse's arm. She keeps her mind exercised by reading, even if it's only the front of a newspaper or a few pages of a novel.

Sometimes a friend calls by, always with food — a cake or a dish of something home-made for supper. They make tea for her, talk for a while, then leave, promising to return in a few days. She enjoys their visits, but they tire her out, and she always sleeps afterwards. Jason finds himself watching her like a hawk, checking every day for signs of her illness worsening. Every day, he or Alice pops in after work. Sometimes they stay to eat with her, sometimes she's asleep when they call by. They bring flowers, books and magazines, and if she's asleep they write her a note for when she wakes.

The carers stay for two weeks each, alternating with each other. They're cancer nurses, specialists in palliative care. They're gentle and kind, staying out of the way when it's clear Dawn needs to rest or have some time with Jason and Alice. They get on with their jobs quietly and efficiently. At first Dawn objected to having a carer stay in the house, but the consultant was adamant.

"These medications are strong," she said. "You may feel dizzy at times. You don't want to risk falling, not at this stage — your bones will be weakened by the medication. I'm afraid it means you can't be on your own in the house overnight — and with this regime of medication, you need support to make sure you're taking the right dose at the right time."

Dawn had no choice but to accept the arrangement. But when she first got home, she made it quite clear that she didn't want any fuss.

"I've lived on my own for a long time now," she said. "It'll be strange enough having someone else in the house. For the moment, I'm fine. I don't want you two worrying about me."

"But—"

"But nothing, Jason. Both of you have jobs, and you can't neglect them. I'm sure I'll need you more soon enough, but for the moment the nurse will look after me. Pop in after work, by all means — I'll be very happy to see you. But don't take time off for me. It'll only make me feel guilty."

It becomes clear that she has prepared for her death from the moment she had the diagnosis. When Jason asks if she needs to review her will, she says: "It's done, Jason. I sorted it out straight away. It's all with my lawyer. There's a box file in the cupboard in the sitting room with the details of what I want for the funeral and so on." He starts to get up, but she says, "No, leave it for the moment, it'll only make you feel bad. But in that file is a form called 'In the event of my death'. It's got everything you need — contact details for friends, suppliers, things you'll need to cancel. I've thought of everything — I hope so anyway. It'll save you that horrible process I went through with your gran, sorting everything out."

This conversation fills him with sadness. Even now she's looking after him, trying to protect him from the worst of the aftermath. He turns away to hide his grief.

He still can't believe what's happening. In a matter of weeks, or months if they're lucky, she'll no longer be there in the house where Jason grew up, holding the fort, supporting him whenever he needs it. Alice says he's grieving already, and he should let his emotions run their course, not try to resist. But sometimes, particularly at night when he can't sleep, the tears run down his cheeks into the pillow and he can't stop them. The feeling of desolation is almost unbearable.

Alice is grieving too, though in a different way. He can see the sorrow in her eyes when she looks at his mum's sleeping face. But she reasons that the two people supporting Dawn can't be sad all the time, not when there's so little time left. She buys a smart speaker and sets it up in Dawn's sitting room, close to the conservatory. Such a practical gift, and one Jason wouldn't have thought of. She brings delicious, tempting treats, and there are always fresh flowers in the house. Luckily, since Carl left, there's been no further sign of the gang, and they can focus on Dawn — for the moment, at least.

"What you're doing for Mum is brilliant," he tells her. "It's fantastic. I can't thank you enough."

She laughs. "You don't need to thank me at all. Anyone would do the same."

"No, they wouldn't."

"It's what partners are for," she says.

"I don't know how I ever managed without you." He takes her face in his hands. "And to think I almost lost you. I'm a fool and I don't deserve you."

"Don't be daft. You'd do the same for me, I know you would. Probably more." She smiles and turns away.

He means it, though. She was right about Carl, and he was wrong. He should have listened to her.

CHAPTER 60

Jason

He thinks about Carl as little as possible, filling his mind and his time with work and his mother. On the few occasions when his mind flits back to that night, the thought triggers a shock reaction. His stomach lurches, his scalp tingles, nausea rises. When he sees a police car, his heart does a sickening backflip. But each time, the car slides past, the officer in the driver's seat staring ahead.

Sometimes he remembers to be vigilant, watching for darkened car windows, unusual activity in the street. But he doesn't want to think about it, not now. Now that there's so little time.

Alice thinks about it too. She checks the papers every week for news of the post-mortem, calls Julie in case Carl's been in touch.

Jason's glad Carl's not here. He has no time for him now.

One evening, on the way to his mum's house, he drops into the newsagent to buy her a paper and some chocolate. There's a queue at the till and he flicks idly through the pages as he waits. His eyes alight on a small headline and he starts reading without paying much attention. But then he almost drops the paper.

"Wimbledon builder's death from natural causes: coroner's verdict."

He reads it again. Graham Needham, a builder from Wimbledon, died of natural causes — a heart attack. No mention of a break-in, or of the money.

The relief is almost overwhelming. Though he hasn't been conscious of thinking much about it, the anxiety has penetrated far into his psyche. A strangled groan escapes from his throat. The woman in front of him turns, startled.

"Sorry," he mumbles. "It's okay."

He breathes deeply. Natural causes. Thank God. He calls Alice, leaving a message on her voicemail. That's one positive piece of news in all this mess.

Should he try to tell Carl? He'll want to know that Needham wasn't murdered — at least they can't be found guilty of that. It'll be a relief to him, too. But then he gets to thinking about how Carl took off, leaving him to take the consequences — and the anger bubbles up again. Forget Carl. He has far more important things to think about.

Tonight his mum is more than usually sleepy, dozing in the late sunshine in the conservatory. He places the chocolate and the newspaper beside her and drops a kiss onto her cheek.

"Mum, you look exhausted. I told you not to dig the garden. Honestly, you won't listen to sense, will you?"

She manages a crooked smile, enjoying his gentle ribbing. They both knew she couldn't possibly manage gardening. "I only did the two flowerbeds. Oh, and I dug up the apple tree, it was getting too big." Her eyelids close, as if the effort of talking has worn her out.

"No wonder you're shattered. Listen, I won't stay — I don't want to tire you out even more. When you wake up, there's a paper and your favourite chocolate, right here."

But she's already asleep.

He kisses her forehead. The carer, Jane, is in the kitchen preparing food. She spoons small amounts into plastic boxes for the freezer. She looks up and smiles.

"Is she eating well?" he asks.

"Not too bad. Some days better than others."

"She seems really sleepy tonight."

"Her body's fighting the cancer — it takes a lot out of her. The drugs don't help, either. But she's had a peaceful day. She's been quite cheerful, watching the birds in the garden. She sat outside for a little while, and seemed to enjoy that." She pauses to stack some boxes into the freezer drawer. "How are you holding up?"

Jason shrugs. When people ask him that question, he struggles to answer. "I'm okay, thanks. Well, I'll be off then. See you tomorrow?"

"Yes, I'm here again tomorrow. I'll look after her, try not to worry too much. She's doing well."

If only that were true.

CHAPTER 61

Alice

I unpack the shopping, glad to be home before the light fades. I love this time of year, when the evenings are growing longer. With the daylight I feel stronger, more positive.

When I called the police for an update, DS Bennett was unavailable. After a few minutes being passed to and fro, I spoke to another officer "on the team".

"Can I ask — what is your interest in the case?"

"We — that is, me and my partner, Jason Green, we were followed by some men. They'd been watching our house. It seemed obvious to us that they knew Jason and Carl were friends. We reported it . . ."

"Ah, wait a moment." There's a long pause. "Yes. Jason Green and Alice Mayfield?"

"Yes, that's us. We'd like to know if there has been any progress on finding Carl's — Mr Jackson's — attackers."

"We're pursuing enquiries. I'm afraid I can't say much more, but we are making progress."

"When you — one of your colleagues — spoke to my partner, the name Neville was mentioned. Are they a

189

suspect?" I'm pushing my luck, but I might just get the answer I'm looking for.

"I'm not able to discuss our enquiries, as you know."

The standard response — disappointing, to say the least.

I try a different tack. "Are you able to tell me if you're actively looking for Mr Jackson?"

"Ah, let me check . . ."

There's some rustling on the line as I wait. After a few moments, the man returns. "We've been in touch with the UK Border Force to ascertain if Mr Jackson has left the country, but they've found nothing so far. It's possible he's using a false passport. Europol and Interpol have been informed."

"How likely is it they'll track him down?"

"Hard to say, I'm afraid. If he doesn't want to be found, then it will be difficult."

* * *

I open the back door and wander onto the terrace, enjoying the sun on my face. Perhaps I can sit out here for a few minutes before starting supper. I go back in and put the kettle on to boil, pulling a mug from the cupboard above, a carton of milk from the fridge.

Behind me, the doorbell rings. I sigh. Jason's always forgetting his keys these days, distracted by everything that's going on.

I open the door with a smile, ready to tease him about his memory. But it's not Jason. Two men are on the doorstep. The first, a tall man with short dark hair, wears a smart black coat and a smile, the other is in jeans and a leather jacket. He's stocky and bald, with tattoos on his neck, and he looks a lot less friendly.

"Hello, Alice," the first man says. "We're looking for someone, and we think you might know where he is."

My heart pounds. I make a sudden move to close the door, but the one in front steps forward to block the doorway. I have no option but to back away, and in an instant they're inside.

"Hey!"

But the first guy is already striding down the hallway towards the kitchen, his heels clicking on the floor tiles. The second one kicks the front door closed behind him, turns me by the shoulders and pushes me in front of him. His fingers dig into my back as I stumble down the hall.

In the kitchen, the man in the coat closes the back door. He turns towards me, still smiling, but it's more like a leer now. His friend is right behind me, blocking my retreat. I can hear his breathing, harsh and throaty, at my shoulder.

"Right," the first man says. "You're going to help us. Tell us what we need to know and you won't get hurt."

"I don't—"

He takes a step towards me. I shrink back, turning my face away from his, acutely aware of the man behind me. There's nothing I can do — they have me in a vice.

"I think you can help us," the smiling man says. "And you'll be glad you did. Where's Jackson?"

I shake my head. "Jackson?"

He grabs my shirt by the collar, forcing my face into his. The smell of his aftershave turns my stomach. I twist away from him but he holds fast.

His eyes are deepest, darkest blue, and evil. He shakes me and I stumble, tripping over the feet of the man behind. "Don't give me that — we know you know him. Carl Jackson. He owes us, and you're going to tell us where he is, or we'll take what we need from you. And your poncey boyfriend. Now, where's Jackson?"

"I don't know. He took off. We don't know where he's gone. Nobody knows."

"Don't give me that!" He gives me another shake and pushes me into a chair, pulling another from the kitchen table. He draws it close, his face inches from mine. With one hand he strokes my hair. I swallow, repulsed — and in an instant he has me by the ponytail, dragging my head to one side. I cry out in pain, my body twisting to ease the pull on my hair.

I want to stay strong, but I'm terrified. There's a sudden rushing in my ears, sweat on the palms of my hands. I hope I'm not going to faint.

"It's the truth — I haven't seen him. He — he was in hospital, then he disappeared."

He frowns and sits back, releasing my hair. He stretches his long legs either side of me, his head on one side, assessing me. I use the moment to take a deep breath. I must do something here, not cave in like a scared cat. But I need him to think I'm too frightened to move.

"Where's your boyfriend?" He uses the word like an insult.

"W-work," I stammer. His fist strikes the table so hard the plates on the sideboard clatter. I flinch, gasping. His hand is like a hammer, the fingers bunched over gold rings, ready to punch.

"Work? Work? Right, then." He leers, his eyes travelling down my body in a blatant expression of power. I recoil, hunching away from him, hiding my body. "No problem. We'll sit and wait for him to come home then, shall we? He'll know where that little bastard is, they're mates, aren't they? We'll get it out of him."

My mind works. What time did Jason say he'd be home? Did he say he'd be late? I don't think so. I can't let him walk into the trap. I have to warn him. Think, think. What can I do? The kitchen knives are across the room, too far to lunge for. These brutes would overpower me in an instant. What else? The second man has stayed in the doorway to the kitchen and is further from me than before. Come on, what can I do?

CHAPTER 62

He was lumbering up the stairway towards me — I could hear his laboured breathing from where I stood, frozen to the floor.

I had no alternative. If I couldn't get out — if he stopped me, everything was lost. This was the only way.

His cheeks were flushed from the drink, his eyes sunken, blood-shot. Panting with the effort of climbing the stairs, it took him a few moments to register me standing there. When he did, he recoiled. His body tensed, his eyes bulged, an angry rash crept up his flaccid neck. The acrid smell of whisky drifted towards me. After what seemed like a lifetime he lunged forward.

"What the — Hey! Give me that bag! Come here . . ."

I crouched as if to spring at him. He tottered towards me, his face scarlet with fury. Only a few feet of carpet between us. I had no weapon, though I tightened my grip on the torch in my right hand, as if it might help somehow. I remember thinking: I might have a chance to overpower an ageing, overweight drunkard. And if I can get past him, I'm pretty sure I can outrun him.

He came towards me, arms outstretched as if to grab my neck. I ducked and kneed him in the groin, hard. I don't know where I found the strength, or the courage. I suppose the adrenaline kicked in — I was desperate. Adrenaline is a wonderful thing, I discovered. A hormone that gives you strength to fight, or to flee — or in my case, both. Clever.

He went down like a tall tree in a forest — from standing to prostrate, no bending anywhere on his body. Once he was down, he started making gurgling noises, groaning, his hands gesticulating. This wasn't the fall, or even the blow in the balls. Despite myself, I hesitated.

His cheeks were the colour of ripe tomatoes. A purple tinge grew around his mouth, foam flecking his lips. He clutched his chest with his left hand. "Ambulance," he croaked. "Call . . ."

I felt sorry for him. But this was my opportunity and I had to take it.

CHAPTER 63

Alice

The smart man sighs. He stands and removes his coat, revealing a tight blue shirt tucked into black trousers, muscles on his arms bulging through the thin fabric. A thick gold chain hangs around his neck. I imagine taking hold of it and twisting it until he cries for mercy. But I don't have a hope.

"You'd be advised to talk, you know. We've got all the time in the world. Might have to stay the night at this rate."

I stifle a gasp. Even my legs are shaking. My hopes of staying strong are shrinking fast.

He laughs in my face, his aftershave sickening me again. "Don't worry, love. I'm a good catch, me — all the girls are begging for it."

He cups his genitals, a lewd expression on his face. "I'm looking forward to it."

His mate guffaws.

I close my eyes, then open them, letting him see the fear. A sob escapes — it's a real one, but I let it go for his benefit. He pulls a pouch and some cigarette papers from a pocket, tobacco spilling to the floor around him. Flicking a speck from his trousers, he starts to roll a cigarette. He has long fingernails, clean and shiny. "Want one?"

I turn my head away. His mate says, "I'll have one, Pete, mate. To pass the time, you know? Got any booze in the house?"

I shake my head, my heart beating so hard I can barely hear. This could get much, much worse.

A strident, urgent note electrifies the room. My mobile, on the worktop, buzzes and jumps. I almost fall off my chair with fright, while the man in the shirt drops the roll-up. He curses, leans down — and I take my chance. Leaping to one side, I grab the kettle and hurl it at his face with one sweep of my arm. He's off-balance, still reaching for the floor as it catches him on the side of the head, scalding-hot water splashing. I don't hesitate. His screams follow me as I wrestle the back door open and burst into the garden.

There's a curse behind me, heavy footsteps running, a shout. But I know where I'm going. There's no back gate, but there is a way over the fence if you know where to look — a tree stump you can put one foot on to give you leverage. I've never done it before — I only know about it because I cleared the ivy off the back fence not long ago — and I'm not sure I'll make it. But fear gives me wings. Without hesitation, I plant one foot on the stump and leap for the fence, straddling it in one, feeling no pain as I drop to the other side. The footsteps pound behind me, then falter as they reach the fence. Curses fill the air as I sprint down the footpath.

At the end of the narrow path, I cannon onto the pavement, almost flattening a passing pedestrian. The figure sways, its arms flailing, as my shoulder hits it hard in the chest. I nearly fall, the momentum driving me forward, my legs unable to stop. The person grabs my arm as I try to right myself.

"Alice!" I can hear the shock in his voice.

I slow — but there's no time to explain. "Jason — run!" He understands in an instant and together we race along the street, into the next one, round the corner and into a small park. We stop behind a tall hedge, panting uncontrollably. I double up, my chest heaving. It's a few minutes before either of us can speak.

"Did we lose them?" I whisper.

"I think so. What happened?" Jason peers through the hedge but it's too dense. We sink to the ground.

"They were waiting for you to get home. I said we didn't know where he'd gone but they didn't believe me. I was so scared, Jason." Now that I'm safe, the tears begin to flow. I wipe them away with my fingers.

He holds me close as I tell him what happened. "I'm sorry, Alice. If only I'd been there."

"It would have been worse if you had — you'd have taken a beating, for sure."

"We need to call the police." He pulls out his mobile and dials with shaking fingers. "Police, please. DS Bennett." There's a pause and he strides about, keeping his eyes on me. "My partner's been attacked. She escaped, yes. They were in the house . . ." He explains briefly what happened.

"What now?" I say as he finishes the call. "We can't go back there until we know they've gone."

"The cops are going there now, don't worry."

But the panic's rising in my chest. "But what if they break the place up? I've left my bag, my phone, everything. Laptop, credit cards, passport — oh, Jason . . ." I'm shaking.

He puts an arm around me again. "We'll get it sorted. You're safe now."

"God, I wish this was all over! We can't live like this, it's terrifying."

I make a silent vow to talk to the police again, to tell them what I know about Carl and the money. They have to find Carl. He is the key to all this, and without his help, we'll never be free.

CHAPTER 64

Jason

They've barely been back ten minutes when Jason's mobile pings. The message stands out as if someone's used a highlighter. It's from Alice.

But Alice is right there in the house — and her phone was taken.

We know where you live. We have your number. We're coming for you. Now, tomorrow, next week, next year. We're coming.

Then: *You have a lovely girlfriend.*

Jason feels the blood drain from his face.

The police officers are outside, checking for signs of the intruders. He steps into the garden and shows the screen to one of the officers.

"This arrived. From Alice's mobile."

The uniformed man nods and takes the handset. "We'll check where that message came from. We'll have to take your phone, I'm afraid."

Alice, appearing at the back door, notices the officer placing Jason's mobile in an evidence bag. "Why's he taking your phone?"

"They messaged me from your mobile. Threatening us."

"Bastards. Now we'll both have to get new ones. Lucky we still have a land line."

"Found anything else missing?"

"Not that I could see. I don't think they went upstairs. All the drawers downstairs were open, but nothing in the bedroom seems to have been touched. They took my bag, my laptop and the passports. I'll have to cancel all my cards. We'll have to change the locks . . ." There's a note of panic in her voice.

"Don't worry about all that. It won't take long. Let's work out what we need to do tonight—"

The officer interjects. "Sir, can I give you some advice for tonight? I suggest you call an emergency locksmith — hang on, I'll give you a card — and get those locks sorted out. You need to secure the house, even if you decide not to stay here for the moment."

Alice looks questioningly at Jason, then back to the officer. "You mean — should we stay in a hotel, or with friends?"

"It's up to you, of course. As long as you get the locks changed, you should be okay."

"Thanks — I'll call the locksmith now." Jason starts for the back door.

"I–I suppose you can't stay around, at least until the locks are done?" Alice says to the officer, a slight wobble in her voice.

"We'll be here for at least another hour, unless something urgent comes up — we need to complete the paperwork. That can take a while," the officer says, with a hint of a smile. "And DS Bennett is on his way. He'd like a chat with you."

CHAPTER 65

Alice

"Let me run through this again," DS Bennett says. He's a stereotypical cop — forties, neat salt-and-pepper hair, pressed trousers. But he's polite, and his gaze is intelligent. "You believe the intruders were after Carl Jackson — for the money he owes." He checks his notes. "They've already been to your door and chased you down the street. Now they've come into your house, uninvited, and threatened you."

We both nod.

"And they've been to Mrs Jackson's house, looking for Carl," Jason adds. "And don't forget the lump of concrete through the window and the dead cat."

"And the message on the wall," I remind him.

DS Bennett nods. "Indeed. And the reason they're threatening you is that Jackson's told them you—" he points his pen at Jason — "can get the money he owes them. And that's not true."

We say "Right" in unison. I bite my lip.

"Why would he do that, though? Put you in the frame, in danger? You're his friend, aren't you?"

Jason shrugs. "To get them off his back, to give them another focus, I don't know. Carl's like that."

To force you to steal the money with him. I try to delete that thought.

"Did you recognise either of the men who came here today?"

I glance at Jason. "I did — yes. The bald one — he came to my door."

"And the people who chased you?" DS Bennett looks at Jason.

"We don't know — it was dark, and I ran when they started to get out of the car," Jason says.

"You didn't see their faces either?" The DS looks at me again. I shake my head. I'm beginning to have some respect for DS Bennett. His eyes bore through me, as if he can see what I'm thinking. It's good that he can't, because I can't get my mind off the bungled heist, the dead man. I glance at Jason. He's nervous as hell, his right leg twitching, a muscle in his cheek working. I can only hope DS Bennett thinks it's all down to the trauma of tonight's events.

His face is inscrutable. He takes a deep breath and lets it out slowly, without lifting his eyes from his notes. Jason and I exchange glances.

DS Bennett lifts his gaze, first to Jason, then to me. "And neither of you has any idea who these people might be?"

Straight away, Jason says, "No idea."

I hesitate. DS Bennett holds my gaze. "Ms Mayfield?"

Jason looks at me in surprise.

I take a deep breath. "It's just — one of your officers asked us — asked Jason — if he'd heard the name Neville. It was in relation to Carl's beating. It's a name I know — from my past — and I know the family still lives around here."

"From your past?"

"I was at school — primary school — with Pete Neville. My father knew his dad, Jack. My dad's name is George Mayfield. That probably doesn't ring a bell, but . . ." I explain, very briefly, about my father and his criminal record. I think this is the first time in my life I've told anyone apart from Jason. "Carl knew Pete Neville, too — they were the same age. They hung out together."

"Do they know who you are?"

"I don't know — I don't think so. Are they in the frame for Carl's beating?"

He thinks for a moment. "We know them, of course. The name comes up on a regular basis in relation to all sorts of crimes around here. We've been trying to catch them for years — but they're smart. There never seems to be any conclusive evidence to nail them. If there was, even for the smallest infringement, we could bring them in and we'd have the chance to get more on them. Jack, his sons, and the rest of them. And yes, we've been keeping an eye on them. Do you have reason to believe it was them who attacked Carl Jackson?"

I shake my head. "It was your officer who put the name into my head."

CHAPTER 66

Alice

"So, Pete Neville was the boy who told everyone your dad was in prison?"

For a long time, I couldn't bring myself to say his name. This is the first time Jason has heard it from me.

"He was. And his dad, Jack Neville, was Dad's mate — the one who got away when Dad went to prison."

"And . . . did Carl borrow from them? Are they the ones threatening us?"

The police have left now, including DS Bennett, and we have new locks front and back. We have chains on the doors and the name of a burglar alarm company to call in the morning. We've just spent an eye-watering amount of money, and it's three in the morning. I'm shattered and I have a thumping headache. All I want to do is to sleep — and for all this to go away.

"I don't know. Could be. It would figure, for sure." I shudder. "Just the sound of their name gives me the horrors."

"I get it, you know. But you can talk to me."

"I know, sorry." I open my mouth to tell him about my visit to Dad, and what I learned. But for some reason I don't.

Partly because I don't know if it's important, partly because I don't want to add to Jason's burden. "I'm so tired, I can't think straight. Let's talk tomorrow."

That time when Jason first spoke to the police — when he told them Carl owed the money and they asked if he knew the name Neville, everything fell into place for me. Carl knew Pete Neville, of course he did. He often hung about with his bully-gang after school, in the park and at the shopping centre. From junior school, right through his teens. Whenever I came across them, I'd walk away, covering any distance to avoid them. Sometimes I'd run, just to get a long way from that boy. I kept my eyes open at all times, because I was terrified of him.

It was well known then that Pete's dad was wealthy — he drove flash cars, was always throwing money around. It was common knowledge that he was dodgy, and when my father started to drink with him at the pub, my mum was horrified. But there wasn't much she could do about it.

It all blew up, of course, when their "business" partnership went horribly wrong. When my dad came out of prison, Mum wasn't having any nonsense, and Dad was too ashamed — or too browbeaten — to argue. As soon as me and my sister had finished school and left home, she insisted they had to move away, and I'm sure it was partly to get Dad from under Jack Neville's influence.

When I went to see Dad, I didn't have a plan in mind. I just wanted to know more about the Neville family, to find out if they were still around, to learn what I could about them. I suspected they might be the ones threatening Carl, but I couldn't be sure.

Then, when they shoved their way into my house, the bald man's mate called him "Pete". That's when I knew I had to do something.

CHAPTER 67

Jason

"I know you don't want chemotherapy or any kind of invasive procedure," the doctor says. "But why suffer when you don't need to?"

"I don't want to become a zombie, that's why. I want to keep my wits about me for as long as possible." Dawn's eyes are still bright, her mind sharp, though she sleeps more and more each day. But the pain seems to be getting worse.

"There's no risk of that, I promise." The doctor writes a note. "We'll make sure we get the balance right, so you keep your marbles for as long as possible."

"That's all I ask."

"It does mean another scan, as soon as we can get one."

"I'll take you," Jason says, and Dawn nods.

"Good. You'll need someone with you," the doctor says. "We'll make sure there's minimal waiting around. When you get to the front of the hospital, stop at the dropping-off point and ask for a wheelchair. Someone will take your mother in, and you can meet her inside once you've parked."

His mother is fading, disappearing before their eyes. Sometimes it seems she's hardly there, the edges of her body blending in with the faded furniture. They've moved her down to the conservatory now, and though she still gets up and dresses occasionally, mostly she stays in bed, moving only to go to the bathroom. The only visitors she can cope with are Jason and Alice. The friends and neighbours leave gifts of food or flowers at the door.

She's beginning to find reading difficult. They take it in turns to read to her, sometimes getting carried away in a story only to look up and find she's asleep. When they're not around, she listens to the radio, and Jason has moved a small television into the corner of the room. She lies propped up on her pillows, watching as birds flit around the garden. Often a smile drifts across her face as she dozes.

They've agreed not to say anything to her about Alice's horrible experience. The last thing they want is for her to worry. She needs peace, and rest, and reassurance that her family will be safe and well when she goes.

* * *

When the results of the scan come in, the consultant calls Jason to the hospital. They're not planning to tell Dawn the meaning of the results, but they need him to know.

"The cancer has spread, as we expected," the consultant says. "Both lungs are now affected, the lymph glands too, and there's evidence of kidney and liver damage. It's slower than we thought, but nonetheless . . ."

"What can we expect?"

"When it spreads to the brain, it becomes terminal. That could be in three to four weeks, but it may take her before then. She's very frail now, as you know, and it wouldn't take much. I'm very sorry."

"It's okay. It's what we were expecting." Though he is prepared for this, his eyes sting with tears. "I don't want her to suffer."

"We'll do our best to keep her comfortable. In the later stages, we'll give her morphine, but we're not there yet. We'll keep a close eye on her. If you have any questions, don't hesitate to ask." She pushes her chair back, a signal that the consultation is over.

"Thank you." Jason stands, his legs barely holding him. Outside the room, in a bare, empty corridor, he stands for a long time, his forehead against the cool wall.

CHAPTER 68

Jason

At her front door, Julie folds him in her arms. "Jason, I've been thinking about you. How's your mum?"

He's thankful for her warmth. "Frail. Not too long, the consultant says."

"Oh, Jason."

"Yeah. But she's in no pain at the moment. I'm glad of that."

"Come in, sit down for a minute."

In the kitchen, she hands him a glass of water. After the hospital visit, it's all he can stomach. With everything that's been going on, he's lost interest in food.

Julie's quick to notice. "You're getting thin, Jason. Are you looking after yourself, and that lovely girl of yours?"

"We're fine. It's not easy, but we've got it under control. Listen, I'm sorry to keep asking, but have you heard anything from Carl? Any idea where he is now?"

Her face brightens. "I had a text yesterday, as it happens. He didn't say much, except he's still in Spain and doing okay. He's got bar work, he said."

That sounds like Carl. "Sunning himself on a beach right now, I suppose."

Jason wonders for a moment if he should tell her what happened to Alice but decides against it. "I'm just being cautious, but the bad guys could still be looking for him. If you see anything suspicious, don't hesitate to call me — or the police, will you?"

"Of course. But I still don't know what it was all about," she says. "Do you have any idea what Carl did to make them do it? I can't believe it was a random attack."

He shakes his head. It's not his secret to tell, and Julie isn't the person to confide in. "I hadn't seen Carl in years when he turned up at our house. He didn't say much about what he'd been up to."

She turns away, a distant look on her face, as if revisiting a distant memory. "I hope he's not causing you any trouble."

"No, honestly, it's fine."

"I mean, after what he did to you as a lad. He should be ashamed of himself."

It takes him a moment to absorb her words. "I'm not — sorry, what do you mean? He saved my life."

A look of concern passes over Julie's face. "You didn't know? But surely—"

He stares at her. "Didn't know what?"

"I'm such an idiot. I'm so sorry, Jason. I wouldn't have brought it up now if I thought you didn't know. He saved your life — but he also caused the accident."

"I'm sorry?" Jason's not sure he heard right. "He caused it? But I thought he saved me."

"He did."

"I'm confused. I slipped on the rocks. That's what he told me, anyway. How could he have caused the accident?"

Julie sighs. "I don't know what got into him. Well, you know what he's like — I can't make any excuses for him. He said you'd been goading each other and he was angry with you. You were up a dangerous path — you got stuck and needed a hand. He reached down to you, but instead of helping you he pushed you backwards — into the river."

CHAPTER 69

Jason knew nothing of the drama that unfolded that day after he reached up for Carl's hand. Only what Carl told him, which, it turns out, was just part of the story.

The boys, stranded on the rocks above, could only watch in horror as the roiling water claimed him. "Jason!" Carl screamed.

"Call for help — quick!" Carl yelled, scrambling down, slipping and sliding, grazing his hands as he tried to get some kind of grip on the rocks. Almost getting swept away himself, he gained the riverbank and raced onto the path, smashing through puddles, almost blinded by the rain. He could still see Jason's body, thrown around by the current, the grey of his hoodie pale against the dark water. He yelled his name, over and over, as he ran, interspersing it with cries of "Help!" in the hope that someone, anyone, would hear him.

But there was no help. He shielded his eyes, searching the river for somewhere to reach Jason — but it was hopeless, he could see nothing through the rain and the darkness. He ran faster, faster. His only hope was to beat the torrent and overtake Jason's floating body. After what seemed like miles, the river narrowed, and a bridge appeared in front of him. This was his chance! The path took him right to the edge of the water as it curved round the wall of the bridge, and at last he was able to see without rain blurring his sight.

Jason's inert body was already sliding past — in a moment he would be gone, beyond Carl's reach. He didn't hesitate. One arm on the riverbank, his hand grasping at clumps of grass, he launched his body into the freezing water. The power of the flow overwhelmed him, he lost his footing and went under. But his foot found something solid to launch him back up, and he rose, spluttering and gasping. Jason's body was almost within reach. "Jason!" he screamed, launching himself forward, his legs kicking wildly, his arms reaching. One hand made contact with Jason's hood and gripped. He drew Jason towards him, grabbed his chin and lifted it up, kicking out with all his strength for the riverbank.

Later, when he looked back on that dark day, he couldn't imagine how he did it. He remembered grasping at mud, at weeds, slipping and stumbling on the soft riverbed. Somehow, he reached the bank. It took all his strength to drag Jason out of the river and he lay on the path for seconds, gasping and spluttering. But he knew he had to check Jason's breathing before it was too late. Taking hold of his shoulders, he hauled the dead weight to the shelter of the bridge, crawling the last few metres on his knees through the clinging mud.

They'd done a life-saving class at school, but all he remembered was the chest compressions and counting. So that's what he did, though he had no idea if he was doing it right. But after what seemed like a lifetime, Jason coughed and vomited. He was alive. Carl collapsed against the bridge, exhausted.

His memory of hauling Jason's unconscious body up to the road was a blur. The mile he had to walk seemed like a hundred, before a car stopped and a voice said: "Need some help there?" He must have passed out then, because he remembered nothing until he woke up in hospital with his mum beside him.

CHAPTER 70

Jason

Jason's incredulous after Julie has finished talking. "He told you all this willingly?"

"No, not willingly. I don't think he'd have confessed to it at all if he hadn't been weak with exhaustion. He was almost delirious when I saw him at the hospital. He sobbed, clinging to me, saying your name over and over. I suspected there was more to it than met the eye and I made him tell me. I had to promise not to tell anyone. I'm sorry, Jason, I thought after all this time, you would know."

All those years of feeling beholden to Carl because he saved his life. Sticking up for him, defending him, taking the rap on his behalf. What a fool he's been. All this — this mess he's in because of his loyalty to Carl — should never have happened. He burns with anger — with Carl for being such a manipulative, selfish person, and with himself for not seeing it.

Somehow, he holds the fury inside, for Julie's sake.

He takes a deep breath. "I didn't know, but it doesn't make a lot of difference now. He saved my life, didn't he? I'm grateful to him for that."

"At least he's done one unselfish thing in his life." A look of deep sadness passes across Julie's face.

"He's not a bad person, Julie. He wasn't trying to kill me."

She sighs. "I suppose we can give him that."

"Indeed." Jason hesitates. "I really need to talk to him, though."

"I can give you the last number he called from, but I don't know if he's moving on, or if he's changing phones." She pulls a mobile from her bag and taps. "Here you go."

He copies the number into his mobile — a new one, since the police still haven't returned his other one. This time, to be safe, he got burner phones for himself and Alice. "Thanks, Julie."

"Let me know how he is, if you manage to get him, won't you?"

"Of course."

CHAPTER 71

Alice

I'm not the least bit surprised when Jason tells me. They were kids, after all, and taking risks was very much in Carl's nature. Jason should have known. It's the exploitation of his better nature that irks me. For all those years after the accident, right up until now, Carl played on Jason's sense of gratitude, allowing him to think that he saved him, without admitting it was his fault in the first place. It's despicable.

"Carl isn't what you'd call a friend, at all — he's scheming, selfish and dishonest. He always was. You can see that now, can't you?"

Jason nods. "When Julie told me, I was furious. If he'd been there, I don't know what I'd have done. But now all I feel is contempt."

"We've got to persuade him to come back. He's the only one who knows who they are — the only one with a chance to get them arrested. He has to talk to the cops now."

Jason passes me his phone.

* * *

I call many times over the next few days. There's no reply. I imagine Carl seeing a number he doesn't recognise, blocking the call. Then, one evening on the way home from the station it connects. There's a long pause.

"Who's this?"

"Carl, it's Alice. Don't cut me off."

"Alice." I hear the anger in his voice. "You shouldn't be calling me." From the sounds in the background, he's out somewhere, and from his breathing, he's walking fast. The hum of traffic muffles his voice, the words fading as a taxicab growls past.

"You need to come back, Carl." The words are barely out of my mouth when I register what I'm hearing. "Wait a minute — are you in London?" No other taxi in the world makes that sound.

"I . . . I might be."

"You are, aren't you, Carl?" I'm incredulous. "Have you been here all along? Never mind — listen, I've got to see you. Where are you now?"

"No! I can't meet you, it's too dangerous."

"Listen, Carl — whoever you owe that money to — they're after us now. They came to the house, they threatened me. I'm terrified, Carl!" My voice rises. "I need to see you, right now. If you don't, I — I'll tell the police everything you've done. I'll go straight there, now, if you won't meet me. Believe me, I will — I'm not kidding."

"Okay, okay. Meet me under the railway bridge in half an hour. Make sure you're not followed." The line goes dead.

I know the place he means; it's not far. I walk fast, making turns into unfamiliar roads before I'm sure there's nobody behind me.

Few people come here. The track has been out of use and neglected for years now, the banks choked with weeds and litter. In the shadows of the railway bridge, a hooded figure stands, slouched against the wall, cigarette smoke curling into the air around him.

Carl scowls at me. "What do you want from me?"

I step towards him. "Is it the Nevilles, Carl?"

He flinches. "What? What are you talking about?"

But I can see from his face that I'm right.

"It is, isn't it? Don't try and fool me, Carl. Was it the Nevilles you borrowed money from? Did they beat you up?"

He nods. "I've known them a long time. Didn't think they'd do this to me."

I close my eyes and appeal to the heavens. But there's no point in trying to tell him.

"The police need proof. They can put them away for a long time for what they've done to you. You need to help them do that."

Carl snorts. "How? How am I supposed to do that?"

"Identify them."

He shakes his head, takes a deep drag from the roll-up in his hand. His fingers shake.

"Carl — they're not going to stop until they find you. Have you thought about that? They'll follow you for ever, wherever you go. You'll never be free — and neither will we if you don't help."

"I can't, Alice. I can't go to the police, they'll bang me up. And the Nevilles will get me in the nick."

"To be honest, Carl, I don't give a stuff about what happens to you, and neither does Jason. But when it comes to my family, I'll do anything to protect them."

Carl's voice hardens. "It's only a hundred grand. Those guys make ten times that in a week. It's nothing to them, you know. They'll calm down."

I can hardly believe my ears. "If you think that, then you're way more stupid than I imagined."

"Don't tell the police, Alice," he says. "I'm in enough shit as it is." His tone is wheedling, pathetic.

I feel a jolt of pure fury. Carl isn't going to play the victim this time, not with me.

"Can you identify them — the blokes who attacked you?"

Carl hesitates. "I–I can't do that."

"Can't — or won't?"

"It's too dangerous."

"You must, Carl! All the cops need is proof. They've been after them for years, only they need evidence. You can give them that. They'll lock them up and we'll all be a lot safer. You'll get protection—"

Carl cuts in, a hard edge to his voice. "Alice, listen to me — I'm not doing it. I gotta go." He throws his cigarette to the ground, mashes it with his heel and starts to walk away.

I grab his arm. "Think about your mum, Carl! They could get to her at any time. What would that do to her?"

He tries to shake me off, but I grip even tighter. "You've got to help us, Carl!"

But he's stronger than me. After a brief tussle, he pulls free and is gone, leaving me alone in the damp shadows of the railway bridge.

CHAPTER 72

I sat on the carpeted floor, my back against the wall, and watched him as he died. I could never have explained away my presence in his house — and anyway, I was carrying a bag full to the brim with stolen money. He would have shopped me in a moment, had he been able to form the words.

Bit by bit the life trickled from his body. After a while — I can't tell you how long — the twitching in his arms slowed, his legs lay limp and heavy. His lips stopped trying to form words and the gurgling sound in his throat slowed and went silent. His eyes, which had stared at me in pure fury for what seemed like a lifetime, ceased to bore into me. I expected his eyelids to flutter and close but they didn't. As his limbs relaxed, so did his face. The life simply drained from his eyes, the fury turned to blankness, and he left.

For a few minutes I was numb, unable to move. But I had to get out of there — more than ever now. I retraced my steps, creeping below the windows, listening at every step. Down the stairs, along the back corridor, to the side door. In the garden, I put the clothes I'd discarded over my black outfit. Back to being an eccentric, limping person with a stick and an old gardening hat. The gates opened automatically, and I slipped out into the dark street, walking slowly towards the station. All I had to do then was wait for the first train of the day.

At home, I packed my clothes into a bin bag to go to the charity shop. The walking stick was going to the same place. The bag of money went into a suitcase under the bed.

Exhausted, I climbed between the cold sheets and fell into a deep, dreamless sleep.

CHAPTER 73

Jason

It's two days until the funeral and Jason is a few minutes from home, walking back from his mum's. Preoccupied with all that's going on, he hunches into his jacket, barely noticing where he's going.

A thump on his shoulder jolts him out of his daze. He curses inwardly at his carelessness and steps back instinctively, almost stumbling into the hedge behind him.

"You — you're coming with me." The voice rasps in his ear as a huge fist grabs him by the arm. A bald head too close to his face, tattoos on the thick neck. A dark-coloured car waiting in the street, its engine running. He smells stale sweat, sees traces of food caught in the man's teeth as he snarls at him. He recoils, pulling his head back, thorns digging into his back as he tries to twist free.

"Wait — wait," he yells as he's dragged towards the car.

"We've waited long enough. Pay up or pay the price."

Jason's losing the battle. He lunges to one side, his flailing hands grabbing hold of a street sign in desperation. But the heavier man is overpowering him, his fingers like iron hooks, digging into the flesh of his arm.

"Just — just hold on," Jason says, speaking fast. "I know you want the money, and I'm getting it—"

"Just get in the car."

Jason's being forced forward, and though he resists with all his strength, it all seems hopeless. In that instant, he's struck by a deep sense of sadness that he won't be able to lay his mum to rest.

"Oi! Oi you, yes, you — what's going on?"

A huge roar splits the air, like the cry of an angry bear. Both men's heads jerk up. Jason almost faints with relief. It's a familiar voice — the neighbour from across the road. He's a plumber, a big man you wouldn't want to mess with — and he's bearing down on them. The bald man drops Jason's arm like a stone.

"All right, Jason?" the neighbour says, stepping between Jason and his attacker, who retreats rapidly to the car, slamming the open door as he goes. With an angry revving, the car races off down the street, leaving Jason and his rescuer staring after it.

"I am now," Jason says, panting. "Thank you so much. I was in trouble there for a moment."

"I don't know what that was all about. But you don't need that kind of shit right now, do you? If he comes around again, you just give me a shout." A huge hand pats him on the shoulder. "I heard about your mum, and I'm sorry for your loss."

"Th-thank you," Jason stammers again.

"No worries at all. You look out for yourself." With a wave, the man is gone, leaving Jason standing on the pavement, weak with relief.

CHAPTER 74

Jason

He stares unseeingly through the window. The street outside is quiet, the parked cars empty and silent, as many of them will be until the weekend. A postman hurries from house to house on the opposite side, gates clanging, a clump of letters and parcels in his hand.

"Come on, Jason, we don't want to be late."

Alice's arms encircle him from behind. She follows his gaze into the street, and he knows she's checking for signs of danger. He sighs. Even on a day like today, they're not safe. In his grief, he's put it to the back of his mind, but he knows Alice hasn't. He turns and holds her tight.

"You can do this," she says.

He inhales. "I know. But saying goodbye is hard."

"It's not really goodbye. She'll still be here, in our hearts."

He's too choked to speak.

The funeral is at the local crematorium, a few minutes' drive from their house. He last went there for his father's funeral, and he remembers it as a soulless, unremarkable building, flanked by a car park. In the Garden of

Remembrance beyond the main building, flowers provided a cacophony of colour in a display that seemed out of keeping with the concept of eternal peace.

Two weeks before her death, Dawn took his hand as he sat beside her bed, pulling him towards her.

"My dear, Jason," she whispered, a look of urgency on her face.

"Mum, what is it?" He leaned in to hear her better.

Her eyes were wide, the blue of her irises fading like the autumn sky.

"It's not going to be long now — no, I know it, and I'm prepared." He had opened his mouth to object but closed it again.

"Please don't grieve when I'm gone. Oh, I know you will, but you have a life to live and a wonderful partner to support you, and you need to look forwards. Wherever I'm going, I'll look out for you, as I've always done. But, Jason — always be you, won't you? Don't be ground down by life, whatever it might throw at you. I'm proud of you. You're strong, and honest and kind, and that's all I ever wanted you to be."

"Mum, I hope you'll always be proud of me, whatever happens, and wherever you are. I want to say—" He swallowed the lump growing fast in his throat. "Thank you, Mum, for being there."

She waved a weak arm. "Now don't get all sentimental on me, it won't do either of us any good. Peppermint tea would be nice . . ." The effort of speaking exhausted her and her eyes were closing as Jason left the room to put the kettle on. He needed that moment to contain the tears.

Not long now. Not long enough to say all the things he wanted to say.

* * *

"Come on, then." Alice takes his arm. He smiles down at her. His mum was right, Alice is the best. He couldn't have got through the last few weeks without her. She lessened the burden, took the strain from his shoulders, by being there for him. It wasn't easy for her, either — her own parents are ageing, and her father's been ill with diabetes for a year or so. She must have been thinking of them when she looked at Dawn, slowly fading away.

Jason vows to make it up to her once all this is over.

At the service, his mind drifts back to the last couple of months. Such a short time since his mum fell ill. It went too fast — one minute she was energetic and full of life, the next close to death, unable to rise from her bed. Too fast, too much. Everything happened at speed, like a film on fast-forward. The world changed; the ground shifted beneath his feet. The only thing holding him solid was Alice.

As the final music plays and people start to leave, he stays in his seat, nodding to Alice to go ahead. The dark-suited man beckons him forward. He knows there's a time limit, but he needs one last moment with his mum. The man nods and gestures towards the coffin.

"Love you, Mum." He places a hand onto the smooth wood. "I won't let you down."

Outside, the sun shines warm on his back as he greets friends and family. There's no sign of any strangers in the crowd, no bald-headed man lurking as he looks around.

He notices for the first time that the crematorium has been renovated — it's clean and modern, the grounds dotted with colourful flowerbeds, framed by shrubs and trees. It's a beautiful place to say goodbye, and he's glad. Dawn would have liked it.

Later, when they have the strength, they'll spread her ashes in her garden, according to her wishes.

Back at the house, the wake goes by in a mist of chatter, laughter and memories.

When the last few stragglers have left, they take mugs of tea into the garden. They sit for a while in comfortable silence with their thoughts.

"I'm glad that's over." Alice sighs. "I think she'd have liked it."

"It was perfect, just what she wanted."

"You're going to miss her terribly. So am I. But we have happy memories, don't we?"

"We do." Jason looks around. The garden he played in, the same flowerbeds, the apple tree that's grown gnarled and old, but keeps on giving every year. The house behind them, carrying all the memories of both parents, of his childhood, of Alice when they first met. It's as if the memories are absorbed into the furniture, the walls, the foundations of this building. "There's so much of my life in this house. I suppose we'll need to sort it all out now, and decide what to do with it," he says. "I'm not looking forward to that."

"I'll help," Alice says. "There'll be lots of decisions to make." She pauses. "Have you thought about moving here, Jason?"

He has, of course. But he's made no decisions. He takes her hand. "It's an option, and there's nothing wrong with it. It's been in the family for a long time — my grandparents lived here, it's where I was born. It would certainly be a wrench to have to sell it, but let's see what we think when the dust settles."

"There's no hurry."

"Luckily. I'll have to apply for probate first. It can take a few months, maybe longer, if it's complex. Though I don't see any reason why it should be."

If Dawn's will is anything like her funeral instructions, it will be crystal clear.

"She certainly knew what she wanted. But she wouldn't want us to feel obliged, if we didn't like the idea of living here."

Alice looks out over the garden. "Why wouldn't we?"

CHAPTER 75

Jason

Dawn's will brings no surprises. Everything passes to Jason, to do with as he wishes.

The surprise — or rather, the shock that shakes the ground beneath him — comes later.

One Saturday, the doorbell rings.

"I'll go," he shouts up the stairs to Alice, who's painting the bathroom in preparation for putting their house on the market. They've decided to move into Dawn's house.

Through the stained glass in the door, he can see the red jacket of the local postman.

"Registered letter for you. I need a signature, please." The postman thrusts a gadget into his hand.

"Great, thank you." He scrawls an illegible signature on the screen and accepts a sturdy envelope.

Intrigued, he studies it as he closes the door. The frank at the top shows it's from Dawn's solicitor — but having not long ago received probate, he was expecting nothing more from him. It's a padded envelope, with something small and hard in the centre.

He takes it through to the kitchen and opens it with a pair of scissors. There's a typed letter inside and another envelope, sealed over thick contents. The hard item is within the second envelope, and Jason's name is typed on the outside, along with the words: CONFIDENTIAL. ONLY TO BE OPENED BY THE ADDRESSEE.

The first letter says simply:

Dear Mr Green,

I hope you are well.

Now that probate has been granted in accordance with your mother's will, I am tasked with sending you the enclosed sealed letter from your mother. Her instructions were to wait until this moment before sending it, securely, to you. It is to be opened by you, and you alone, and it is your decision as to whether you want to share the contents with anyone else. Neither I nor any of my colleagues has any knowledge of those contents.

I wish you well.
Best regards,
John McReady,
Senior Partner
McReady and McReady
Solicitors

CHAPTER 76

Jason

At the bottom of the garden, sitting on the tree stump beside the shed, he opens the second letter, his stomach fluttering. In the envelope are many pages of notepaper. Both sides of each sheet are covered with Dawn's handwriting, neat and clear, and at the end of the letter is a key, securely taped to the paper.

It's an odd feeling, seeing her handwriting on the page, as fresh as if it was written yesterday. He has the sensation that his mum is right there, standing over him while he reads.

The contents of the letter are even stranger.

My dear Jason,

By now, if things have gone as planned, you will have received probate on my will. So I imagine this moment is more than six months after my death.

What follows on the next pages is going to be a shock, for which I'm truly sorry. I've written it all down in some detail. Hopefully I've answered many of the questions that you'll have when I tell you what happened in the months before I died. My objective was to save you and Alice from a terrible situation that seemed as if it would never be resolved — and I knew I was the only person who could get away with it.

I only had a few weeks left, and my physical strength was beginning to trickle away. You and Alice had your whole lives ahead of you, and yet you were about to ruin all that opportunity and potential for the one person who had let you down constantly since you were a young boy.

I hope you forgive me for what I'm about to tell you. More than that, I hope it solves your problem, and his, once and for all.

Here is my story.

It was easy, as it turned out — much easier than I expected.

First, I went shopping. I found some of the things I needed in the charity shop. The rest came from a place selling toys and gadgets.

I made myself look very ordinary. I wore scruffy jeans, my oldest jacket, a scarf round my neck and a gardening hat with a floppy brim. Carrying a walking stick and a small backpack, I travelled by tube to Wimbledon and found the street. There, I made my way slowly up and down the pavement, limping slightly. Outside the house, I pretended to have a long conversation on my mobile. That way I could check out the front of the house through the gates without suspicion . . .

There are many pages to the story and every one leaves Jason stunned. He has to keep going back to reread. The final page leaves him breathless.

So, there you are. Your mother is — was — a murderer. Or as good as. I left the poor man having a heart attack, without so much as a comforting hand on his forehead. More to the point, I didn't call an ambulance. I thought about it, but as it was, the police wouldn't even know he had been burgled — if I'd done everything right — and why arouse suspicion? If someone called the police, it would mean they'd been in the house, and I wasn't going to risk it.

So be it, and I'm sorry to leave you with that thought.

But I knew I was going to die soon, and I had to stop you ruining your life. If Alice couldn't persuade you not to do it, I knew I'd have very little chance. You've always been stubborn in your loyalty to Carl, and I respect that. It's misguided, but I respect it.

Alice told me everything — all about Carl's mad plan. You mustn't be angry with her for that. She was deeply worried about you and desperate to talk to someone. But I came up with the idea alone. She would have locked me up rather than let me do it. I would probably have done the same in her place.

I figured I had very little to lose. Though I didn't want to die in prison, I reckoned the chances of saving you were high enough to make it worth the risk. I didn't think about failure. When you have nothing to lose, it's easier — you worry less, somehow.

I still can't quite believe I did it. After a lifetime of being an honest, upstanding human being with a rock-solid set of values, I carried out a serious crime — and succeeded. In a strange way, I'm rather proud of myself. Carl should have come to me for help, not you. No ropes and pulleys, just common sense, diligent research and patience. But those are qualities Carl will never have.

The key attached to this letter is precious. Don't lose it, it's the only one. In my shed, beneath the rather horrible mess in the back left-hand corner, is an old metal box, securely locked. It used to be your father's, and it's perfect for this job. The key will open it. Inside, you'll find a large amount of cash. I haven't counted it all, but I know it's more than £100,000.

The money represents the proceeds of a crime, and I know you'll feel uncomfortable with that. Nonetheless, I want you to give Carl the money to pay off his debt. He doesn't deserve it, but that's why I took it, after all. The idea of you and Alice looking over your shoulders for the rest of your lives is unbearable. This way, I've sorted his problem out once and for all, and you have no reason to be loyal to him ever again. You will owe him nothing after this, remember that. I suggest you don't give him more than he owes, but the decision is yours.

The rest belongs to you. I would prefer you not to give it away, but if you want to, go ahead — I won't know. If you keep it, you can put it aside for your children — yours and Alice's, I hope. I'm sad that I won't see them, or you and Alice as parents, but there's nothing I can do about that. I'm sure they'll grow into wonderful people, like both of you, and will give you as much joy as you gave to me. Make sure they have a picture of me, won't you? I'd like to think they've seen my face.

I hope there's a way to watch you from wherever I'm going. If there is, I'll find it!

You're a lovely person, Jason, and I want nothing to change that. I'm proud of you, and I love you. Have the best life. Mum xx

CHAPTER 77

Jason

With shaking fingers, he removes the key from the last page of the letter, puts it back in the envelope and stuffs it into the pocket of his jeans.

At their house, he calls up the stairs. "Going over to Mum's, won't be long." Without waiting for Alice's answer, he leaves the house, forcing his trembling legs to walk towards Dawn's house.

It's too much to take in. His mother — his mum — staid, upstanding, honest Dawn — *she* stole the money? He wouldn't have believed it in a million years — and he can't believe it now. Surely it's not true? Had she lost her mind at the end of her life, to have written a letter like that? Could it be a complete fabrication? Yet there it was, every moment of her incredible feat described in black and white, with an ordinary ballpoint pen on ordinary white paper. He could almost hear her voice in each perfectly formed sentence — matter-of-fact, objective, practical. *This is what happened, son, and I'm telling you in this way so you'll know it's true.*

He barely notices the pavement beneath his feet, and it's a surprise when he reaches the house. Time seems to have sped by since he opened the envelope.

It's all so bizarre. Did he imagine the letter? Was he asleep, dozing, in that strange state where you're half-awake and dreaming? But the letter's still in his back pocket, the key to the box now in his hand.

His heart rate soars when he reaches the shed, beating impossibly fast. He stops for a moment to breathe, forcing his pulse to slow. It would be ironic — crazy — if he dropped dead in the act of finding a huge stash of money left to him by his terminally ill mother, who stole it from a bent builder who died in front of her. Oh, and by the way, the bent builder was his wayward best friend's father. Nobody would believe it.

The box is well hidden over in the far corner, on the dusty floor. It's covered with an old towel, on which empty flower pots and garden tools lie in a heap. The sense of anticipation is almost unbearable as he crouches down to sweep away the mess. And there is the rusty metal box.

The key slides smoothly into place. He opens the lid, removes a layer of plastic sheeting — and gasps. He sinks back onto his heels, his eyes riveted on the contents.

There is the evidence.

Sheaves of purple notes sit neatly side by side, looking as if they arrived today, fresh from the Royal Mint. Beneath them, a row the same, only red. Pile after pile after pile.

"Oh, my God," he whispers. "Omigod, omigod. Mum, you really did it, didn't you?"

He sits gaping at the money for a few moments, letting Dawn's words sink in. Then he rolls onto his back in the dust, the dried mud and the cobwebs of the shed floor and laughs, a straight-from-the-belly guffaw that spreads through his entire body, shaking him into a helpless heap. He laughs until tears stream from his eyes and his limbs feel like jelly, until all the tension that's held him together for months has seeped away.

CHAPTER 78

Alice

"It's not true. It isn't." It's all I'm capable of saying.

Jason's just back from Dawn's house. He's shown me the extraordinary letter from his mum and the sheaves of fifty-pound notes. I would never have believed it if he hadn't shown them to me.

"I know. I was utterly floored when I read it," he says. "I had absolutely no idea she'd done it, and I still wouldn't believe it, except . . . Here's the proof. And the letter is perfectly written. She knew exactly what she was doing when she wrote it — and when she stole the money." He shakes his head for about the hundredth time. "Who knew she had it in her? I certainly didn't."

"Nor me — I never would have thought it possible. We knew she was a strong person — but this! And she was ill, weakened by the cancer, when she did it. Unbelievable."

There's a long silence as we gaze at the money. It still doesn't look real. It's like Monopoly money, part of a story, an imaginary game. We'll put it away in a minute and forget about it until next time.

I put out a tentative hand, take a sheaf of notes. I count it aloud. I start on the next. When I've got up to one thousand pounds, I take a look at the sheaf and measure it against the next. Jason watches me, mesmerised. I get to fifty thousand pounds in what seems like moments — and it's a remarkably small pile.

"Huh," I say, gazing at it. "There you go. A hundred thousand is double that size. If there's any left over, it's yours, to do with as you wish. Isn't that what she said?"

Jason stares. "But — is that the right thing to do? It's not our money, is it?"

"It wasn't Needham's either. I think we should do as your mum asks."

"I don't know, Alice. I'm in shock. I can't work out what's right and what's wrong."

But I can see this clearly. "Think about it, Jason. Do you want to explain to the police everything that happened? Why your mum decided to steal the money? That you and Carl were going to take it, but your plan was pre-empted by your sick mother, because she couldn't bear for you to have a bunch of criminals looking down your neck?"

He shakes his head again.

"Good luck with that, if you do. No, we should carry out her wishes. Otherwise, it will all have been for nothing, won't it? Your mum died knowing that she'd stood by while someone died in front of her, and I can't imagine what that did to her. And it was all to save you. You and me."

The scale of Dawn's sacrifice is jaw-dropping. She would never have left someone to die, it was against every principle she lived for. But she was determined to head off disaster, to stop Jason from making the biggest mistake of his life, and to free him and me from years of suspicion and fear. She found a way, even though it meant breaking all her rules. It would be ungrateful — unconscionable, even — not to do as she asks.

"I think she pulled off something quite miraculous." My fingers riffle through the pile of banknotes.

"So do I, believe me, but I still can't believe it."

"Well, you'd better, because we've got a huge stack of notes staring us in the face, and it won't leave us alone until it's gone, out of the house, out of our possession, into Carl's hands and beyond."

"You're right. I need some time to process it, that's all. We'll lock it in the shed for the moment, like she did."

"What, our shed?" I'm horrified that he could even think about keeping it here.

"Why not?"

"It's a terrible idea," I say, shuddering. "I won't sleep with it there, you know I won't. Already I feel like it's burning a hole in the table. There's so much energy coming from that pile, you could run the heating off it for a whole year. And what if those guys come back? They could—" I don't even want to think about what they could do to us if they come back.

"Don't worry, I'll deal with it. I'll take it back to Mum's shed. I don't want you to be stressed over it."

I don't want to stress over it, either. The money is hot in a hundred different ways. It can't stay in either house for long. We'll have to decide what to do with it. Fast.

CHAPTER 79

Alice

"What now?" We sit, staring at each other, Dawn's letter lying on the table between us. The money's back in the shed, but I still feel its energy, as if it's piled right there in front of me.

"I've been asking myself that ever since I saw the money," Jason says. "I can barely take it in — my mind's completely blank."

Mine isn't much better, but I try to think logically. "We can't put it in the bank, not even for a few days. They'll think we're money-launderers or something. The taxman would be on our backs before we knew it. Anyway, your mum did what she did to get us out of this mess, so that's what we're going to do."

"But how?"

"Carl has to pay off the debt with this money, and we have to make sure it happens. It's the only way we'll be in the clear. Jason?"

He looks sick at the thought.

"When I think of Carl now, all I feel is disgust. But you're right, we have to do this."

"I'll do it." All I want is for it to end, for us to be free.

"What?" Jason seems startled. "Why would you want to do that? You don't even like him."

"All the more reason for me to do it. I'll tell him we have the money and I'll make sure he pays it back. Then he leaves us alone. For ever."

He hesitates for a moment. "No. I mean, it would be great to dodge the responsibility. But selfish. It's tempting, and I'm grateful — but I can't let you. It should be me."

"Why? You owe him nothing, Jason."

"No, not because of him. Because of my mum, and what she did for me. And because it could be risky." He puts his head in his hands. It's becoming a habit.

I reach to him over the table. "Look, Jason, it's easier for me. I have no feelings for him — except perhaps contempt."

"Yes, and I might punch him on the nose if I see him."

I scoff. "You haven't done anything like that in your entire life. Look — we'll do it together. Two heads are better than one, after all, and if we do have to take a risk, we can look out for each other."

"Okay, we'll do it together. If you're sure?"

"I am. Let's look at our options." I think rapidly. "We can't trust Carl to take the money and pay off his debt, can we?"

"Definitely not."

"We'll have to do it with him." I shudder. Even the thought of seeing those men again terrifies me.

"Carl will have to tell us how to contact them."

"If we can drag him there."

CHAPTER 80

Alice

"Julie, sorry, but — I need to get in touch with Carl again."

"I'm waiting for him to call."

"I really need to speak to him. If he calls, could you give him a message from me, please? And Julie — I'm sorry but — please don't ask me what it's all about because I can't tell you. You don't want to know, believe me."

Julie sighs. "And so it goes on," she says, as if to herself. "Okay, fire away. I'll write it down so I won't forget."

"Can you ask him to call me on this number as soon as he gets the message? Tell him we've found a way to help him."

"Is that it? Call you on this number, and you've found a way to help him? I think I can remember that."

"Exactly that. Also, he needs to be quick, or the opportunity will pass."

"Be quick, or the opportunity will pass . . ."

I can hear a pencil scraping across paper.

"I'd love to ask you what's going on, but—"

"I'm sorry, I really can't."

"I know. Be careful, though. Don't put yourself at risk, will you, Alice?"

"Absolutely not. I'll be in touch."

* * *

It's a long two days before we hear from Carl. In my head, the pile of cash is like dry tinder — I imagine Dawn's shed bursting into flames. I can't wait to get rid of it. Sleep is impossible and I wander around the house like a ghost, unable to settle.

When the phone rings, I nearly jump out of my skin.

I grab it, fingers fumbling, press the speaker icon. I signal to Jason, who comes close.

"Carl," I say, holding my voice steady. "Where are you?"

"It doesn't matter. You have something for me?" Traffic noise and wind blurs his voice, but it's recognisably Carl.

"We've got the money."

"What? Say that again."

"We've got the cash, Carl."

Carl's voice drops to a hoarse whisper. "Really? Did I hear that right — you've got the money?"

I picture him stopping in his tracks, frozen with astonishment.

"Yes, all of it."

"All of it? How—?"

"You don't need to know. Listen to me carefully. You're going to contact Pete Neville — or whichever one of those villains you've been dealing with. You're going to set up a drop-off point — we'll tell you where. You're going to hand over the money. All of it, the whole hundred grand. And we're going to make sure you do it."

"Wait a minute—"

"Let me talk to him." Jason holds his hand out. I stare in surprise. Only a few moments ago, he swore he couldn't bear to hear his voice.

I mouth: *Are you sure?* But he takes the phone, his mouth set in a hard line.

240

"Carl, it's me. Listen carefully." He keeps his voice loud and firm, enunciating every word. "You have to do this. We have the money. We're giving you the chance to stop all this madness. You pay them off and they'll leave us alone. End of story."

"But—"

Jason cuts him short. "You're going to do this, or we'll take the money to the police and tell them you stole it from Needham. This is not an idle threat — I mean it. Understood? Am I making myself clear?"

"You can't do that, Jason, you—"

"For once in your life, Carl, listen. You got us into this mess and you're going to get us out of it. I don't care what happens to you afterwards. And listen carefully — I'm not doing this for you, I'm doing it for us, for me and Alice, for my mum and yours. You don't deserve my help, after everything you've done. You're a selfish bastard and always have been. After this, I'm done with you."

"Okay, okay—"

"We're going to meet, today, the three of us. You're going to make the call, and we're going to tell you what to say. Now, where are you?"

CHAPTER 81

Alice

Carl looks thinner than ever as he walks towards us. He hunches into a grubby jacket, a cap pulled down over his eyes. He perches on the end of the wooden bench where we sit. He glances over his shoulder, avoiding eye contact.

We're outside a cafe not far from Dawn's house — there's a chilly breeze but it's safer than being indoors, and we can leave at any time. We've already paid for our drinks.

"Carl."

"Jason, Alice." He nods at us. I notice his fingernails: bitten to the quick, misshapen and dirty. Nothing about him looks healthy.

"Get your phone out." Jason's voice could freeze boiling water.

Carl obeys without a word. I notice a slight shake in his fingers; I'm not surprised the strain is showing.

I place a hand on Jason's arm, slowing him down. "Who lent you the money, Carl? We know it's the Nevilles, but who exactly?"

Carl's leg jiggles as he hesitates. "Why do you need to know?"

I ignore the question. "Was it Jack?"

"Nah."

"Pete then."

He nods, his eyes flitting along the street. "I can't hang about—"

I cut in. "What does he look like now, Pete Neville? The last time I saw him he was a skinny teenager."

"Evil-looking bastard. Bald. Overweight, tattoos on his neck. Jason's seen him."

So it was him. "You have his number?"

He nods again. Sunken eyes meet mine for the first time. I remove my hand from Jason's arm.

"Okay, this is what you say," Jason says. "He comes alone. Only him. None of his cronies. He meets you in St James's Park, noon tomorrow, third bench down the main walkway, opposite the sign that says Buckingham Palace. Opposite, okay? You'll be there with the money in a bag. He'll sit next to you, you get up and walk off. He takes the bag and leaves. Got it?"

"Where will you be?"

"Oh, we'll be there, don't worry, watching your every move. Right there, beside you, in front of you, wherever we can keep an eye on you. Don't even think about taking off with the money. You won't get as far as I can throw you."

"I dunno, Jason. I don't like it . . . what if I can't get that seat — if there's someone sitting there already?"

"Don't worry about that. We'll handle the detail."

"Will the cops be there?"

"If they are, it won't be down to us," Jason says. "But if you try anything, anything at all, Carl, I swear . . ."

"Fine. I promise—"

"Don't bother to promise me anything, Carl. Your promises are worthless."

Carl drops his eyes at the naked hostility in Jason's gaze.

"Meet us here tomorrow morning at ten. You'd better not be late."

We watch as Carl's shambling figure hurries out of sight.

CHAPTER 82

Alice

In the park, people are out in numbers — tourists strolling, office workers sitting on benches eating sandwiches. But it's a different kind of busy from the streets nearby. The pace here is slower, green spaces creating pools of peace between the paths. Water birds peck at foliage by the lake's edge or wander across the paths, ignoring people who stop and stare and take pictures on their phones. The squirrels here are so tame they barely move when people approach, only running when children or dogs give chase.

I've been in the park for over an hour, strolling around with a large camera, taking pictures, just like many other people. I blend in well in my jeans and trainers, a baseball cap shading my eyes, stopping every so often to snap the birds. I check my phone every few minutes.

All clear at the moment — I type. Jason sends a thumbs-up in reply.

With half an hour to go, I settle down on the wooden bench, placing the empty camera bag next to me. I rest one arm casually over it. Opposite is the sign for the palace.

Gazing around as if taking in the scenery, I check for likely watchers, but there's nothing obvious. I line up the camera for a shot of some Canada geese strolling along the grass at the edge of the nearby water, but instead of snapping the birds, I take multiple pictures of people coming and going through the park. The camera is borrowed from a friend, a keen photographer. My pictures aren't up to much, but it's not the scenery I'm interested in. I test the lens on Jason and Carl, lurking by the water's edge. I can see their faces in some detail from quite a distance.

Though we've planned this carefully, I'm tense with nerves. We're amateurs at this kind of thing, and I'm terrified it might go wrong. It was hard to search for "*How to do a secret drop of one hundred thousand pounds to a dangerous criminal gang — safely — without the police*" — though we did try. The only information I could find was related to kidnappers and a swap — almost always involving the police. The one thing I did learn was it's best to do the drop in a public place, where even the Nevilles might think twice about violence.

We agreed there was no way we could trust Carl with the money, not even for a moment, so we had to be here in person. But we wanted him to be the "face" of the handover, rather than us. We reasoned he started it, so he must end it.

Jason carries the money in a backpack strapped to his front, like I've seen tourists do for safety. It must be burning a hole in his chest. I breathe deeply but my heart's racing. Only a few minutes to go and we'll be shot of the money, of Carl — for ever, with a bit of luck. I scan knots of approaching people, searching for Pete Neville — the man who forced his way into our house and threatened me. I would never have imagined he was the boy I used to know, apart from being a nasty piece of work. People change a lot, though. Skinny teenage boys become potbellied, balding men, unrecognisable from their schoolboy photos.

All clear, I think.

I watch through the camera as Jason and Carl leave their spot and stroll towards me. Jason looks around, one hand on Carl's shoulder in what looks like a friendly gesture, while Carl stays hunched, a hood over his head, gazing at the ground. He's not liking this any more than we are. When they reach the bench, they ignore me. I look up, my hand moving the camera bag to my lap. They sit, the bag on the bench between them.

I stand slowly, begin to walk away. That's when I see him.

Pete Neville is walking towards me, his eyes travelling beyond me to Jason and Carl. The man at my door, the leering intruder in my kitchen.

He hasn't seen me, and though my heart's pounding out of my chest, I carry on walking until he's passed by. Then I swing around, apologising to a couple whose path I've crossed, and stop by a tree. I need to see this, take pictures. If he turns, he'll see me, but I'm hoping I'll look like just another tourist with a camera. It's Carl he's focused on, and the bag. Jason has scooted to the other end of the bench, leaving enough space for someone to sit between him and the bag.

At that moment, a pelican strolls across the pathway not far from the bench, attracting a knot of people pointing and exclaiming, taking pictures on their mobiles. For a moment, my view is obscured. I step forward, craning my neck to see — but when the crowd parts for an instant, the bench is empty. No Jason, no Carl, no Neville.

No bag.

Panicking, I look one way, then the other, but I can't see much beyond the pelican and the crowd of people. I run to the bench — there's no sign of any of them.

I let out a cry of anguish, attracting looks from passers-by. I wave them away and start to run.

CHAPTER 83

Jason

From the moment he saw Carl at the cafe, Jason knew he wasn't going to behave. He could tell from the shifty look in his eyes.

When he sees the bald guy approaching, he takes his hand off the bag for a fraction of a second — but Carl's off in an instant, arms flailing, the bag flying, one strap trailing on the ground behind him. With a curse, Jason gives chase, his feet flying. There's a shout from behind and for a horrible moment he imagines a deafening gunshot. But the crowds provide protection — groups open up or step to one side as the two men run through them. Carl doesn't have a chance — he's malnourished, unhealthy and unfit, and in a matter of moments Jason's on him. He grabs the bag and wrenches it from Carl's hand. A sickening crack splits the air between them.

"You've broken my finger!" Carl cries, bending over to cradle his hand, his breath coming in hoarse, painful gasps. Aware of the people milling around, Jason leans over as if to comfort him, keeping the bag firmly in his grasp. A couple turn to see what's happening. "Everything all right?" the man says.

"Everything's fine," Jason replies and they turn away.

"Well done, Carl," he hisses into Carl's ear. "We had pretty low expectations, but you've hit the depths." He grabs Carl's thin arm, holding him in a vice-like grip as Neville runs up to them, breathing hard. He feels Carl flinch under his hand.

"Caught him," Jason said, holding out the bag. "I believe this belongs to you."

Neville takes the bag, unzips it and rummages around inside for a moment. Jason holds his breath.

Neville looks at him and nods. "Want me to take him off your hands?" He indicates Carl with his head.

"Nah, you're all right. I'll deal with him. Quits then?"

With a nod, the man turns and disappears into the crowds.

CHAPTER 84

Alice

"You can let me go now, can't you?" Carl wheedles as we frogmarch him from the tube station to the car. We kept him close all the way here, flanking him on either side as we sat in silence, holding on to his jacket when we left the train. "You don't need me anymore. It's all done, isn't it?"

"Not quite." Jason pushes him into the back seat of the car as I climb in the other side. The central locking clicks. We're taking no chances with him now.

"Where are you taking me?"

"You'll see soon enough." Jason starts the engine.

When we draw up at the red-brick seventies building with its distinctive blue sign, Carl makes a move for the door. "No, no — I'm not doing this—"

"It's locked. We're going in there, and you're coming with us," Jason says, turning in the driver's seat to look at him.

"You can't do this to me," Carl says, his eyes flashing. "It's kidnapping."

"Try that one on the police then, they're right here," Jason says, indicating the police station. "Or would you like me to do a citizen's arrest on you? I'm sure I could come up with a reason or two."

Carl stares, disbelieving. "You'd do that? After everything we've been through? I thought we were mates . . ."

"Mates don't let each other down, Carl. Remember that, if you ever manage to make another friend."

Disbelief turns to hostility and Carl's mouth twists into an ugly snarl. He's not bothering to hide his dark side now. "Don't play the Angel bloody Gabriel with me, Jason. Where d'you get the money? Was it my dad's?"

So he knew Graham was his father, after all. No wonder he was determined to carry out his plan — he must have reasoned the money was as good as his.

In the rear-view mirror, Jason fixes Carl with a look so intense it could break the glass. "No idea what you're talking about, Carl." Jason opens the door and gets out.

Carl's shoulders slump as Jason walks round to open the door for him. He turns to me. "C'mon, Alice, don't make me do this."

"Believe me, Carl, if I'd had my way, you'd have done it a long time ago. It's no good appealing to me."

It's the first time I've seen DS Bennett smile. "Well, well," he says, turning to Carl. "Looks like you're going to help us catch this crook Neville, then, are you, Mr Jackson? Can't tell you how long we've been waiting for the moment — and how grateful we'll be for your help. Here, go with my colleague — he'll sort out the identification process for you."

A man in jeans and a sweatshirt puts his head around the door and indicates for Carl to follow him. With a last pleading glance at Jason, he leaves the room.

"Thanks for delivering him to us," DS Bennett says, turning to Jason.

"He wasn't keen — we almost had to drag him here," Jason says. "I just hope he'll testify against them. It won't be easy to get him to court."

"That's our problem now. But I think we'll find a way," DS Bennett says.

CHAPTER 85

Alice

I'm almost skipping as we walk out of the station, leaving Carl to his fate. I imagine the interview will be interesting. I wonder how he'll bear up to the questioning, what he'll say to DS Bennett. In due course, we may find out. We may not, and I don't care. For the moment, the job's done.

Carl will identify Neville as his attacker and, if Bennett has his way, testify against him in court. Grievous bodily harm is a serious charge and will mean a long prison sentence. For that alone, Neville will be out of the way for a long time — and if the coppers play their cards right, they may be able to get him for a lot more than that. As for Carl, there'll be plenty of other questions to answer, and he'll have to dig himself out of whatever holes he creates for himself.

"It's done, Jason — we're safe!" I say as we climb into the car. "No more looking over our shoulders, no more sleepless nights. The money's gone, the crooks are off our backs — it's up to the coppers now. Let's hope they do a decent job and bang them all up for a very long time."

Jason gives me a sideways glance. "Do I get the impression you have a smidgen of respect for DS Bennett then?"

I snort. "Maybe."

As I open the front door to our house, relief floods through my veins. My body feels lighter, the air around me fresher. "Perhaps now we can get back to normal — whatever that might be, after all that's happened."

"I suppose so. But are we really safe now?" Jason says. "Can we assume they won't come for us, now they have the money? It seems so long since we felt safe, since we could walk down the street without worrying about who might be following us. It's going to take a while to get out of the habit."

I've been thinking the same thing. "I know. It'll feel good, being free of all that."

"Maybe."

"What, you think they'll still come after us? Why would they, now they've got their money?"

"I don't know, but I'm thinking: Pete Neville's just one of them, isn't he? The big boss is Jack, your dad's old mate — he's still operating, and there must be others. They're a known criminal gang, aren't they? I don't know how these things work, but if the family bears us a grudge for putting Pete in prison, we could still be in trouble."

I squeeze his hand. "I suppose that's possible. But we're not a threat to them, and the debt's been paid. That must mean something, even to villains. Somehow, my instincts tell me everything will be all right now."

"I hope you're right," Jason says. He pauses. "And what's Carl going to say about the money? How will he explain how he got enough to pay them back?"

"I told him exactly what to say. That you lent it to him. Thanks to your mum's will."

"That might work, I suppose."

"It will. If they think further than that, I'll be amazed. They'll be too keen to nab the Nevilles to think that laterally."

"You know what I'm thinking?"

"Wondering what will happen to Carl now?"

"I'm thinking he's going to hate us for dumping him with the police."

I glance at his face. A small smile plays around his mouth.

"You're right," I say. "He'll never forgive us. I doubt we'll ever see him again."

Jason chuckles.

CHAPTER 86

Alice

A few months later, a call comes in on the house phone. Jason picks it up. "Hello?"

A startled look crosses his face as he listens, then recognition. "Yes, of course. What can I do for you?" After a moment, he holds the handset out to me. "DS Bennett. For you," he says.

"DS Bennett," I say. "We weren't expecting to hear from you again so soon. Well, to be honest, not at all." I smile at Jason.

"I wanted to update you," DS Bennett says. "The information you passed on from your father, regarding Jack Neville. It's very interesting. Very interesting indeed. It's taken a while — we had to check everything out, we had to be one hundred per cent certain. But I'm pleased to say — we've got him now. He's in custody, along with two other members of his gang, on remand and awaiting trial. Just wanted to give you the heads-up."

"That's great news," I say. The question mark on Jason's face makes me smile. "My dad will be delighted to hear it. Thank you."

"We should be thanking you. It's taken far too long, but we got there in the end."

"Yes. I'm going to call Dad right away."

I put the phone down with a satisfied sigh.

"Well?" Jason says. "Something I should know?"

"Ah yes. I was going to tell you, but there was so much going on at the time, with your mum and everything else, the Carl situation — I didn't want to bother you with it. I went to see Dad — it was when the cops first mentioned the Nevilles. I wanted to find out what he knew about them. I suspected — no, I knew straight away — it must have been them Carl was tangled up with. Remember I told you Mum always protested that Dad was innocent, that he was led astray by Jack Neville? And she told the police over and over that Dad had conclusive proof against him, but they ignored her?"

"I do remember that."

"Well, it turns out Dad kept the proof. He had a file on his laptop. Names, dates, numbers — the lot. I saved it onto a memory stick and sent it to DS Bennett. It's taken a while, but he's cracked it. Jack Neville's in custody, along with his cronies — and he'll be locked away for a very long time, if Bennett's got anything to do with it."

I want to capture the look on Jason's face and bottle it.

THE END

ACKNOWLEDGEMENTS

A huge thank you to all my writer friends for their support, and to the writing community as a whole. You're one of the kindest groups I've known and without you this job would be truly lonely.

Thanks of course to my lovely editor, Emma Grundy Haigh, for her patience guiding me in the right direction (as always) for this book, and to Clare Coombes for helping me improve it.

Thank you to the wonderful team at Joffe Books — long may you thrive!

Huge respect to my first readers, Judy Jones and my sister, Kate Mercer, for cheerfully ploughing through the many iterations of this novel. I'm not sure it was a rewarding job, but I'm eternally grateful.

Thanks to the Tugboats and to the Marlow Book Club for your kind words and enthusiasm for my work — and to all my friends, my family and my partner.

And finally, of course, to my readers. Without you, I wouldn't be writing.

* * *

A portion of the earnings from this book will be going to Heal Rewilding. Heal is raising money to buy land in England and rewild it, giving land back to nature, forever. Respect and love, Jan and Jeremy! www.healrewilding.org.uk

THE JOFFE BOOKS STORY

We began in 2014 when Jasper agreed to publish his mum's much-rejected romance novel and it became a bestseller.

Since then we've grown into the largest independent publisher in the UK. We're extremely proud to publish some of the very best writers in the world, including Joy Ellis, Faith Martin, Caro Ramsay, Helen Forrester, Simon Brett and Robert Goddard. Everyone at Joffe Books loves reading and we never forget that it all begins with the magic of an author telling a story.

We are proud to publish talented first-time authors, as well as established writers whose books we love introducing to a new generation of readers.

We have been shortlisted for Independent Publisher of the Year at the British Book Awards three times, in 2020, 2021 and 2022, and for the Diversity and Inclusivity Award at the Independent Publishing Awards in 2022.

We built this company with your help, and we love to hear from you, so please email us about absolutely anything bookish at feedback@joffebooks.com

If you want to receive free books every Friday and hear about all our new releases, join our mailing list: www.joffebooks.com/contact

And when you tell your friends about us, just remember: it's pronounced Joffe as in coffee or toffee!

ALSO BY SUSANNA BEARD

STANDALONES
THE PERFECT LIFE
THE GIRL ON THE BEACH
WHAT HAPPENED THAT NIGHT
THE LOST BROTHER
THE PERFECT NEIGHBOUR
THE PERFECT WITNESS
THE BEST FRIEND

Milton Keynes UK
Ingram Content Group UK Ltd.
UKHW041813240823
427439UK00003B/6

9 781835 260166